She was so *losing all perspective here.*

Her sister was missing, could be in just about any awful trouble imaginable. And what about her original problem with Brand? The one of ten years ago. To learn to forgive was one thing.

To want to try again...

Uh-uh. Bad idea. The pinnacle, the absolute summit of dumb.

And she *didn't*. She sincerely did not want to try again with this man.

And yet. All her heart wanted was to stay there— or anywhere, as long as Brand was there with her.

Dumb. Oh yeah. She just needed to say so.

But what she said was, "All right. My house. But only for a few minutes."

His grin widened. "Let's go."

Dear Reader,

Oh, those Bravo men...

Have I said that before? I'm sure I have. How can I help it? It seems to be a Bravo trait to fall head-over-heels for just the right woman—and then come way too close to losing her.

Or just plain *actually* losing her.

Take Brand Bravo. He found the woman for him while still in high school. But he knew he was ill-suited to forever-after. Absolutely certain he was doing the right thing, he left Charlene Cooper behind.

Ten years later and—let us hope—wiser, Brand has finally realized all that he lost. He only wants to try again. Too bad Charlene is having none of him. He'll need a miracle to get back in her good graces—a miracle in the form of a totally unexpected bundle of joy....

Yours always,

Christine

CHRISTINE RIMMER

FROM HERE TO PATERNITY

SPECIAL EDITION®

Published by Silhouette Books

America's Publisher of Contemporary Romance

SILHOUETTE BOOKS

ISBN-13: 978-0-373-24825-4
ISBN-10:   0-373-24825-3

FROM HERE TO PATERNITY

Books by Christine Rimmer

CHRISTINE RIMMER

came to her profession the long way around. Before settling down to write about the magic of romance, she'd been everything, including an actress, a salesclerk and a waitress. Now that she's finally found work that suits her perfectly, she insists she never had a problem keeping a job—she was merely gaining "life experience" for her future as a novelist. Christine is grateful not only for the joy she finds in writing, but also for what waits when the day's work is through: a man she loves, who loves her right back, and the privilege of watching their children grow and change day to day. She lives with her family in Oklahoma. Visit Christine at her new home on the Web at www.christinerimmer.com.

For M.S.R. Love you.
Always.

Chapter One

For Charlene Cooper, that world-shaking Saturday in April began like just about every other Saturday.

The alarm jarred her from sleep at five-fifteen. She rolled out of bed, yawning, and padded straight to the bathroom, where she shrugged out of her sleep shirt, hung it on the back of the bathroom door and climbed in the shower.

Twenty minutes later, she was dressed in jeans and a red T-shirt with the Dixie's Diner logo across the front, her blond hair pinned loosely up in the back. She took a minute or two to brush on a hint of blush, a little lipstick and mascara.

Since her bedroom and the only bath were both

off the front entry, she was ready for work without once having entered her living room or the kitchen beyond. She never ate breakfast before she left in the morning. There would be coffee at the diner, after all. And Teddy, the early-shift cook, would scramble her a couple of eggs on request.

She ducked back into the bedroom to grab her purse from the dresser and returned to the entry, where she reached for the doorknob.

At that exact moment, just before she turned the knob, her life changed forever.

With one tiny sound.

It was a soft, happy, cooing sort of sound. Like a puppy. Or a kitten. Or maybe a pigeon. It was coming from her living room.

A pigeon. In her living room?

There it was again…and no. Not a pigeon. Not an animal at all.

More like a…

Charlene let out a tiny cry of pure bewilderment and whirled for the living room, where she found something truly, completely impossible.

A baby.

A baby all wrapped in a fluffy pink blanket, lying there on her antique mahogany and horsehair sofa, beneath the picture window that looked out on the deck….

A baby.

Charlene's purse hit the rug with a soft plop. She

put her hands over her mouth, backed up to the ancient rocker that had once belonged to her great-grandmother and slowly lowered herself to the seat. The rocker creaked softly as it took her weight.

And the baby on the sofa waved its fat little hands and cooed at the ceiling as if it didn't have a worry in the world. Not far away, on the floor at the end of the sofa, there was a battered-looking flowered diaper bag and a dingy blue car seat.

Somebody had broken into her house and left a baby, complete with car seat and diaper bag. Who would do such a crazy thing?

Slowly, as the baby made a goofy little noise that sounded almost like a giggle, Charlene lowered her hands and gripped the carved arms of the old rocker. "Hello?" she said aloud, her voice all strangled and strange sounding. Maybe the mother—or whoever had brought the baby—was still in the house. She cleared her throat and called more forcefully in the direction of the kitchen and the spare bedroom at the back of it. "Anybody here?"

No answer.

The baby waved its fists some more, and the pink blanket made a rustling sound, a sound like paper crackling....

Charlene shot to her feet again and approached the cooing infant.

There. Pinned to the blanket on the far side. A folded sheet of lined paper.

The baby gurgled and cooed some more, blinking its blue eyes, smiling up at Charlene as if it recognized her.

But that was impossible. This baby was tiny—too tiny to recognize anyone—at that age when they *seemed* to be smiling at you, but weren't, really. No more than they were actually waving at you when they wiggled their fat little arms in the air.

Hands shaking, Charlene unpinned the folded paper. She set the pin in a pinecone bowl on the side table. Her knees felt kind of wobbly, so she backed up again and sat in the rocker before she dared to unfold the lined sheet.

It was wrinkled, the note. She smoothed it on her knee, blinking in horrified disbelief as she recognized that sloppy, back-slanted scrawl.

"Oh, God," she heard herself whisper. "Oh, no..."

Dear Charlene,
Surprise! LOL.
    Meet your niece, Mia Scarlett Cooper. She is five weeks old, born on March 15. Isn't she beautiful? Takes after her mommy that way. And I need a little favor. See. The thing is. It's just not working out for me, dragging a kid around everywhere I go. I need a break, and even though you and me don't always get along on stuff, I know you'll take good care of her. She's a good baby.

And I don't know how to tell you this, but I guess you need to know that Brand is her dad. And in case you're wondering, the answer is yes, that's why I ran away last year. Because of Brand and how he treated me.

With love, even though I bet you don't believe me,
Sissy

Sissy...

Charlene had the strangest feeling, as if she would shatter and fly apart, pieces of her shooting everywhere. Carefully, holding herself together by sheer effort of will, she rose again and approached the child.

The baby—Mia. Her name was Mia—and she didn't seem to be smiling anymore. But she wasn't crying, either. She gazed up at Charlene through wide, calm eyes and went on gently waving those itty-bitty fists.

She had the cutest little dimple in her chin.

A dimple that reminded Charlene of the cleft Brand Bravo had in *his* chin.

"Oh, God..."

Charlene turned and sat on the sofa at the feet of the pink-blanketed bundle. Some time went by. Seconds? Minutes? She couldn't have said. She sat there, unmoving, staring straight ahead at the grouping of family photos on the opposite wall—pictures that included one of her mom and her dad on their wedding day. Her mother was laughing as she stuffed wedding cake into the open mouth of her groom. They looked so happy. Young. Strong in the certainty that they had long lives ahead of them.

There were family groupings of the four of them: father, mother, two smiling daughters. And of Charlene and Sissy—separately and together. In one, Charlene stood on the steps of the big white frame house on Jewel Street, the house where they'd all been a family, before the accident. The child, Charlene, was grinning wide, proudly holding her newborn baby sister in her nine-year-old arms.

"Sissy…" Charlene said the name aloud.

And then she blinked some more, shook her head and read the note again. And again—three times through before her stunned mind could finally encompass the enormity of all this.

Her baby sister had a baby of her own, a baby who just happened to be lying right there beside Charlene, kicking her tiny feet under the blanket, staring up at the slanted, beamed ceiling, making those adorable happy-baby sounds.

A baby named Mia, whose father was…Brand?

No. Charlene couldn't bear to believe that—and really, it just wasn't possible. Was it?

Of course not. He *wouldn't*…

Yes, it was true that she had a low opinion of Mr. Bigshot Lawyer and Confirmed Bachelor, Brand Bravo. Anyone in town could tell you that. Still,

Charlene would have sworn he'd never sink so low as to seduce a mixed-up kid like Sissy, a kid who just happened to be Charlene's own sister.

But then again…

Well, the timing did add up. And last year, during Sissy's disastrous month back in town, she'd grown swiftly notorious. And not only for her skimpy outfits, spiked purple hair and the safety pin she wore in her nose, but also for the way she would throw herself at every guy in sight.

And even if her style was way out there for a conservative community like New Bethlehem Flat, no one could deny that she *was* pretty in her own über-Goth kind of way. It was just possible that she'd caught Brand in a moment of weakness.

"Ga," the baby said. "Wa…"

And what about the way Sissy left last June, vanishing in the middle of the night on the *same* night that someone ransacked Brand's law office and stole his petty cash drawer? The thief had never been caught, but everyone in town—including Charlene, though she'd never admit it out loud—knew it had to be Sissy.

Why would Sissy do that, trash Brand's office, steal the cash drawer and disappear into the middle of the night, unless she was really mad or desperately hurting—or both?

The baby kicked, sharply nudging Charlene's thigh. Charlene instinctively responded, smoothing a hand on the blanket, feeling the shape of that tiny, perfect foot, almost smiling in spite of the shock and confusion she was dealing with.

And besides, she thought, though Sissy had problems—a raft of them—there would be no point in her lying about Brand being the father. Even a messed-up nineteen-year-old has to know that all it takes is a simple paternity test to settle that question once and for all.

So. Well. It had to be true, didn't it?

This baby, her niece, was Brand Bravo's child.

"Oh, no," Charlene whispered and put her head in her hands. "Oh, God, no…"

Chapter Two

Let it never be said that Charlene Cooper didn't take care of business—no matter how impossible and distressing that business might be.

A half hour later, she'd made use of the contents of the diaper bag to feed and change her niece. She'd called Teddy, the cook, and told him she wouldn't be in until later, and she'd found another waitress to open up for her.

She carried Mia into her own room and put her down on the bed, bolstering her with pillows on either side. Then she collected the car seat from the living room and went out to strap it into the backseat of her AWD wagon.

Charlene had zero experience with baby seats, so the process took longer than expected. She read the half-worn-off instructions on the side of the seat and followed them as best she could, feeling edgy and frustrated the whole time, hoping the baby was all right, alone in the house.

Finally, after twenty-five minutes of fiddling with the darn thing, she managed to get it in place and secure. She rushed back inside, where she found Mia right where she'd left her, tucked among the pillows, sound asleep, sucking her tiny thumb.

Those bright blue eyes popped wide for a moment as Charlene picked her up, but then she only snuggled in on Charlene's shoulder and went back to sleep. Same thing when Charlene put her in the car seat. She blinked awake, yawned and promptly dropped off again, her head drooping to the side, the little tufts of peach fuzz on her pink scalp clinging to the musty-looking fabric of the seat cover.

Charlene ran back inside to grab her purse and the diaper bag. She threw them both across the front seat, climbed in behind the wheel and started the engine. At the end of her gravel driveway, she turned right onto Upper Main.

In no time she was driving through the heart of New Bethlehem Flat—known to all who lived there as, simply, the Flat. Resisting the temptation to continue past the diner farther along and make sure her cook and substitute waitress had got the place open all right, she turned left on Commerce Lane and crossed the Deely Bridge, passing Old Tony Dellazola strolling over town on foot as he did every morning at about that time.

Old Tony was one of Charlene's diehard regulars. He spotted her silver-gray wagon going by and frowned, probably thinking that she ought to be at the diner, awaiting his arrival, a full pot of decaf close at hand, ready to make sure Teddy fried up his bacon just right. Charlene pasted on a smile for him, sketched a jaunty wave and drove on, past the Sierra Star Bed and Breakfast—which was run by Brand's mother, Chastity—on the right and the Methodist Church on the left.

Up the street and around the corner, Commerce Lane became the highway. She was heading east out of town, the steep mountain to her left, a sharp cliff dropping down to the river on the right, the occasional bridge providing a way across the swiftly flowing water to the cabins and houses on the other side. She passed the bridge to the Firefly Resort and a second that led across to a series of vacation homes. At the third bridge, which was just wide enough for one car to pass at a time, she turned.

On the far side, she took the road to the left. It was a short ride to the sign that read Bravo. 301 Riverside Road. She turned into the driveway.

The new, chalet-style house appeared before her, nestled attractively among the evergreens. Charlene had never seen it from the driveway side before. It looked kind of cozy and unassuming. From across the river, its soaring walls of windows gleamed and twinkled in the sun, and the wraparound redwood deck was spacious and inviting.

Brand loved his new house. Everyone in town said so.

Charlene had to admit that even from the plainer, driveway side, it was a fine-looking house. Not that it mattered, not that she cared.

She pulled in next to the garage and got the baby out of the back. Mia did a little blinking and squinting at being disturbed, but quickly settled back to sleep, snuffling at Charlene's shoulder, sighing in the sweetest way.

Charlene pushed the door shut. It closed with a tight, final sort of sound. Somewhere in the trees nearby, a woodpecker rat-tat-tatted and a little farther off a mourning dove cried. The air smelled of cedar and of woodsmoke from some nearby cabin's chimney. Above the canopy of pine branches, the morning sky was clear and blue as Mia's eyes.

A beautiful setting, so picturesque and peaceful.

Yet Charlene's pulse raced. Her stomach ached, it was tied in such a tight knot of fury and hurt and unswerving determination.

She followed the stone walk around to the main entrance, on the west side of the house. She marched right up to the big front door and rang the bell.

The sound echoed within.

She waited, gently rocking the sleeping baby in her arms, trying to take slow breaths and think peaceful thoughts. She wanted her mind clear as a mountain spring when he answered, she needed to be logical and calm when she spoke to him.

Through the leaded glass that decorated the top half of the door, she could see a slate-floored entry area, daylight slanting in from a skylight above. No sign of *him,* though.

She shifted the baby a little more firmly on her supporting arm and used her free hand to punch the bell again. That time she rang it longer, pressing her lips tight together in her impatience, pushing on that bell, good and steady for a full count of ten.

Still he didn't come.

Again she pressed it, this time in short bursts.

Apparently, big-shot bachelor lawyers didn't get up at the crack of dawn on Saturdays like a lot of regular folks had to. Well, too bad. She shoved at that bell again, longer and harder and with more determination than ever.

That did it. Finally. He appeared in the entry, scowling and scratching his head, squinting at her through the glass of the door.

Charlene stood straighter and laid a protective hand on Mia's back. The door swung open and he was standing there, droopy-eyed, barely awake, wearing a ratty pair of sweatpants—and nothing else.

His bronze-colored hair stuck out at all angles and there was a sleep mark on his cheek. He looked disgustingly sexy and manly and rumpled.

Not that she cared. She didn't. Not in the least.

"Charlene," he muttered in that warm, lazy, slightly rough voice of his. "What the hell?" He braced a lean arm on the door frame and looked her up and down through low-lidded eyes. "Never thought I'd see *you* come knocking at my door."

She wasn't letting him get to her. She spoke without emotion. "It's important. Let me in." And she didn't wait for him to get out of the way, either, but just pushed right on past him into that handsome sky-lit foyer.

"What's with the baby?" he asked from behind her. "I didn't even know you were pregnant."

"Ha-ha." She cradled Mia all the more tenderly as she turned to look into those fine hazel eyes. "We need to talk."

He scratched his head again and snorted. "I'm dreaming, right? In real life, you haven't spoken to me in ten years."

"This is no dream," she told him smartly, "and you'd better believe it's not."

"Whoa," he said, with far too much good humor. "So, then. Coffee?"

She longed to inform him that she wanted nothing from him, ever. Under any circumstances. But that would be a lie, since she did want something. She wanted him to admit he'd had sex with her sister.

That he'd fathered the sweet child she held in her arms....

She realized she was staring blindly into space when he waved a hand in front of her face. "Charlene. You in there?"

She blinked and focused on the rat in front of her. "Yes. Of course."

"Well, then? Coffee?"

"Yes. Coffee. Fine."

In his huge kitchen, with its top-of-the-line appliances and endless expanses of granite counters, she took a seat at the table, lifting the baby a little higher on her shoulder as she lowered herself to a chair.

He ground coffee and put water in the coffee-maker and slid the pot in place beneath the brewing spout. She said nothing, only waited, until he pushed the brew button and turned to her, leaning back against the counter, folding those big arms of his over his gorgeous bare chest. "Okay. What's up?"

She supported the baby on one arm as she lifted her hip and slid Sissy's note from the front pocket of her jeans.

"What's that?" He looked at her from under his golden brows—not suspicious, exactly, but not eager, either.

"See for yourself." She dropped the folded square

of paper on the table and slapped her palm on it. "There you go."

He watched her for a moment, as if seeking some clue to what might be going on inside her head. Then he shrugged and pushed himself away from the counter.

She listened to the coffeemaker gurgle and drip as he unfolded the paper and stared at the words scrawled there. He stared at them for a long time.

Charlene waited, saying nothing, shifting Mia to her other shoulder, smoothing her blanket, gently rubbing her little back.

Finally he looked up. He shook his head. And then he yanked out the nearest chair and plunked himself in it. He threw the note on the table. "No way. I never touched your sister. I am not the father of that kid."

Charlene glared at him. He glared back at her.

Finally she said wearily, "Now, why did I just know you'd say that?"

He shifted, drawing his bare feet under the chair, leaning his muscular torso her way. "Because it's true? Because, in spite of how much you hate my guts, you know I'm an honest man who doesn't have sex with screwed-up teenagers—and that means you know that baby isn't mine?"

Okay, he had a point. Whatever she might think of him, she'd never doubted his honesty. Not until right now.

She said, "There's no reason for her to accuse you—unless it's true."

He leaned back in the chair. "Come on, Charlene. Get real. It's not as if your crazy little sister needs a *reason* to do the insane stuff she does."

She refused to reply to that. If she did, she knew she would screech at him and call him terrible names. How dare he say that about Sissy?

Even if it did happen to be true.

He glanced away, his hand on the table tightening to a fist. She watched him control himself. When he spoke again, it was softly. Carefully. "Okay. I shouldn't have said that. I realize your sister's a sensitive subject with you."

Sensitive didn't even begin to cover it. She'd always felt so guilty about the way Sissy got sent away after their parents died. She'd fought and fought hard to keep Sissy with her. But she'd been eighteen and single. And the judge had been the kind who thought a nine-year-old would be better off in a two-parent home.

If Brand had only—

But no.

There was no point in going there. That was then and it was over. They needed to talk about what to do now. Still, she couldn't resist getting on him about the more-recent past. "You should never have hired her to work for you last year."

He looked at the note again, touched the edge

of it, pulled his hand away quickly. "I was only trying to help."

She stared at him dead-on and refused to say another word to him until he lifted that golden head and met her eyes. Then she instructed, slowly and clearly, "Do me a favor. Don't help. Ever."

His gaze didn't waver. "Charlene. I know you want to believe the worst of me, but—"

"That's not true!" She said it much too fast and much too loud, as if she were trying to convince herself as much as him. Mia stirred and whimpered.

Brand only shook his head.

Something about that, about the simple denial in the movement, got her fury building again. It would accomplish nothing to start screaming at him. Still, she *burned* to give him a giant-size piece of her mind.

Mia whimpered some more.

Poor little thing. She was probably picking up on the tension Charlene was trying so hard to control.

"Shh. It's okay, honey," Charlene whispered, not looking at Brand, trying to think peaceful thoughts, rocking the baby gently back and forth, rubbing her tiny, warm back. "It's okay…."

Mia sighed and snuggled close again, going loose and limp once more.

The coffeemaker gave a final sputter. Brand rose, went to the counter, filled a pair of mugs and returned to the table. He slid one mug toward her as he sipped from the other.

She ignored the coffee and challenged in a voice she somehow managed to keep low and calm, "So. That's your story, huh? You're insisting this baby isn't yours."

"It's not a story. It's the truth. That is not my baby—and by the way, where's Sissy?"

Exactly the question she didn't want to answer. "Um. What do you mean?"

"You *know* what I mean. How come she sent you here to do her dirty work?"

"Dirty work?" She tried to sound superior and aloof.

"Figure of speech. Where's Sissy?"

"How would I know? You read the note."

He looked down at the wrinkled note again. "You want me to figure the situation out for myself, is that it?" He slanted her a glance. When she refused to respond, he continued, "Okay. I'll take a crack at it. You haven't *seen* Sissy since last year. You haven't even talked to her. She left that baby on your doorstep along with this note. She abandoned her own kid, dropped her off with you and took off again."

It hurt. A lot. To hear him say it right out loud like that. "Not on the doorstep," she argued, sounding ridiculous and knowing she did, taking issue with a minor point to soften the enormous awfulness of what Sissy had done. "Not on the doorstep. On the couch. I...found her there, this morning, on my way out the door."

"You *found* her on the couch?"

"Isn't that what I just said?"

"Sissy broke into your house and abandoned her own baby—but still, you'll take her word against mine."

Mia stirred again. Charlene patted her to soothe her. "Sissy has a key, so she didn't break in. My house is her house, always. And she didn't abandon Mia, either. She left her with me. Sissy knows she can trust me to take good care of her."

Brand gave her a long, level look. "And that makes it all right, somehow, that she abandoned her kid with *you?*"

"Stop saying that word."

"What word? Abandoned?"

"Oh, I could reach right out and slap you silly about now."

For that, all she got was another slow shake of his head.

She counted to three and then said with slow care, "I'm not here to talk about Sissy."

"Getting that. Big and bold as a whole new day."

"Are you denying that Mia is yours?"

"What? You didn't hear me? I denied it five minutes ago, I'm denying it now. I'll always deny it. Because that baby *isn't* mine."

"Then I'll expect you to take a paternity test." She delivered the ultimatum and waited for him to start squirming.

He nodded. "I think that's a good idea. And I want it done right. I don't want there ever to be any question of the results. I want a legally binding test by a reputable lab, strict chain of custody of the DNA samples, so everyone involved is satisfied with the outcome."

She cleared her throat. All right. She had to admit, for a guy who was trying to weasel out of taking responsibility for his child, he seemed pretty eager to get to the truth....

But then, as an attorney, maybe he knew some way to falsify the test results.

Charlene shut her eyes. No. Whatever she thought of him, she didn't believe that. He might be lying to himself, telling himself he couldn't be the father.

But he wouldn't rig the test. He wouldn't stoop that low.

She said, "I want to get going on it right away."

He said, "Good. Get ahold of Sissy, tell her we need a copy of the baby's birth certificate and she'll have to show up at the collection location to sign a permission form to have the test done."

"Uh. The collection location?"

"The lab where you'll take the baby to have the DNA sample collected. It's a simple, quick procedure. They run a cotton swab on the inside of the cheek. Painless."

"But I don't..." She cradled Mia closer, breathed in the sweet baby scent of her skin. "You're saying we need Sissy's permission?"

"Charlene. Think about it. You don't go performing tests on minors without the approval of a parent or a legal guardian."

"Can't we just…have it done?"

"By some fly-by-night lab that sends a kit in the mail? How dependable do you think those results are going to be—let alone how legally binding?"

As much as she hated to admit it, she knew he was right. Oh, what was her problem? What had possessed her to come storming over here? She'd gained nothing for Mia—and she'd given him a chance to say things about Sissy that she really didn't want to hear.

Gently she shifted the baby to her other shoulder. She was stalling. Coming to grips with the fact that she had no choice now but to bust to the bald, ugly truth.

She made herself say it. "You know I can't reach Sissy. I haven't seen or heard from her since she left town last June. She didn't leave me so much as a PO box number, let alone a phone number or an address."

He studied her for moment and then he suggested, "Maybe there's some friend of hers you could call? What about that aunt she went to live with after your parents died?"

Aunt Irma. Dear God. Anyone but her. "It's… doubtful. But I'll check around."

He got up and poured himself some more coffee, turning when the mug was full to lean on the counter again. He sipped. "There's another option."

Why did she get the feeling she was going to hate what he said next? She regarded him sideways. "What option?"

"Call Child Protective Services. Tell them what's happened, explain that your sister has claimed I'm the baby's father. You might be able to get the state to authorize permission for the DNA sample."

She cradled Mia closer. "Call CPS. Uh-uh. No way."

It wasn't right that he knew what she was thinking. But of course, he did. "This is a different situation than ten years ago. You're not eighteen now. You're a grown woman with a business, not to mention a respected and well-liked member of your community."

"I was well liked then. And respected. We had the diner then, to support us. My aunt still managed to take Sissy away—and why are we talking about this?"

"I told you. Because it's an option."

"No. No, it's not. I do not want to mess with Child Protective Services, and you, of all people, ought to know that. I will not give them any chance to take this baby. I am her aunt. She's…visiting. That's how I want it. You understand?"

"Charlene…"

God. Why had she come here? What a stupid, stupid move. Her throat had clutched up with tears of frustration—and fear. She gulped the tears down and commanded, "Don't you dare call CPS on me, Brand Bravo."

He set his mug on the counter and put up both hands, palms out. As if she had a gun on him or something. "Look. Totally your call. But you have to face that CPS might eventually enter the picture."

She would never face such a thing. What had happened to Sissy was never happening to Sissy's child. Carefully cradling the baby with a supporting hand around the back of her tender little head, she stood. "I see now I shouldn't have…rushed over here. My mistake. I was very upset and not thinking clearly. I understand what I'm up against now, though. I see there's no way but to hold off on the paternity test until Sissy's available to sign all the papers."

"Charlene."

She bit her lip and shook her head at him. "Don't."

He hesitated, but in the end he couldn't keep his damn mouth shut. "You've got to ask yourself. What if she's never available?"

Charlene had no intention of asking herself that. Not ever. No matter what. She said firmly, "She *will* be available. She'll come home. Eventually. When she does, be prepared to take that paternity test."

Those muscular shoulders lifted in a shrug. "Fair enough."

She wondered why anyone would ever say that.

Fair enough? As if there was anything about any of this that was fair.

Oh, why had she come here, she asked herself again. She was a thousand different kinds of fool for even talking to Brand.

Was he Mia's father? Had he seduced Sissy last year?

She was no closer to knowing the answer to those questions than she would have been if she'd gone about her business, taken things a little slower, held off on confronting him until she'd had time to think it over and understood the situation better.

She should have been more…reasonable about all this. Not come flying over here at seven in the morning waving poor little Mia in his face, dragging him from bed and hurling accusations at him.

He just…he did that to her. Made her crazy. Made her want to pitch a big, ugly fit.

Ten whole years since he'd ripped out her heart and stomped it flat. And she still hated him, still looked for any opportunity to blame him—for anything.

It wasn't healthy. She had to get past her never-ending anger at him. Somehow.

Soon.

She picked up the note from the table, folded it back to a small square with one hand and stuck it in her pocket again. Then she turned for the door.

Chapter Three

Brand watched her walk out and said nothing. Not see you later. Not even goodbye.

He and Charlene were long past the point where they made polite noises at each other. He and Charlene were…enemies. Or something damn close.

It really bugged him, how much she despised him. He prided himself on being a likable guy.

Yeah. It was kind of a big thing for him, to get along with the people who lived in his town. He'd worked hard to build himself a good reputation. It hadn't been easy. He was a Bravo, after all, one of the apparently numberless bastard sons of the infamous Blake Bravo, who'd been a real bad actor, a man who had kidnapped his own nephew for a fortune in diamonds, done murder at least once and lived on for more than thirty years after the world believed him dead.

Brand had a whole bunch of half brothers, sons of women like his mother, Chastity, who had fallen for Blake Bravo's dangerous bad-guy charm. Chastity had four sons by Blake, two of whom grew up well-known for their wild antics and troublemaking ways. Brand and Brett, Chastity Bravo's two middle sons, did their best to be different, to live normal, noncontroversial lives.

Now Brett was the town doctor, happily married with a new baby son. And Brand had gone into law, moving back to town a couple of years ago to join his retiring uncle Clovis's legal practice.

Brand considered himself successful, a productive member of his community. He knew he shouldn't be the least bothered by some long-ago girlfriend's low opinion of him.

And the fact that he knew he shouldn't be bothered, well, that only bugged him all the more.

But it wasn't his problem. None of it. Not that poor abandoned baby, not Charlene. Not wild, messed-up, provocative Sissy.

And, yeah. That was one thing Charlene had been right about. He never should have hired Sissy to do filing and help out at Cook and Bravo, Attorneys at Law. It had been a blazingly stupid move.

Too bad. He'd hired Charlene's wild little sister, and now he'd be paying the price.

Eventually, the whole mess was bound to sort itself out. He'd take the paternity test when and if Sissy ever showed her face in town again. But for now his part was to stay the hell out of it.

And get on with his own damn life.

Charlene was just pulling out of Brand's driveway when she spotted two local residents, Redonda Beals and Emmy Ralens, out for a morning stroll. They waved as she passed them, and Charlene waved back, being careful to smile as broadly as possible and to look as if she didn't have a care in the world.

Redonda and Emmy were both in their midfifties and best pals, nice ladies who came into the diner often and always tipped generously. They weren't real big on gossip or anything. But everyone in town knew that Charlene Cooper would never be caught dead visiting Brand Bravo—at that fine new house of his or anywhere else for that matter. So the two nice ladies couldn't be blamed for looking slightly puzzled at the sight of Charlene emerging from Brand's driveway.

On the short drive back to town she came to a decision. Instead of turning for home, she headed for the diner. Might as well get it over with, let folks have a look at her niece.

After all, this *was* the Flat. Everybody knew everything about everyone else. Seeing Redonda and

Emmy back there by Brand's house had brought it home to her that there was absolutely no sense in trying to keep the baby hidden away.

Uh-uh. Smarter to play the proud auntie. Let them all know she had absolutely nothing to hide. The building loomed up on her left, the big black-and-white sign with red lettering over the door proclaiming it Dixie's Diner.

At seven-thirty, when Charlene entered with Mia in her arms, the counter was full and so were the booths. Lots of folks liked to come in early for breakfast, and Saturdays were no exception.

Teddy was flipping pancakes on the grill and Rita—the waitress who'd agreed to come in at the last minute—was taking an order from the Winkle family at the back booth. Nan and George Winkle had three boys: twelve, eight and six. They were a rambunctious crew and prone to talking over each other. The boys would order more than they could possibly eat, while Nan and George vetoed and bargained and eventually allowed them to get whatever they wanted.

George, Jr., who had something of a crush on Charlene, waved wildly at the sight of her. "Hey. Charlene. Hi!"

Stevie, the youngest, started bouncing up and down, announcing in a loud sing-song, "Charlene has got a baby, an itty-bitty baby…"

"Shh, now," said Nan. "Just you settle down."

Matt, the middle son, demanded, "I want OJ *and*

hot chocolate. I'll drink 'em both, promise. Swear it. Please, I want both. Please..."

"Son," said George. "Settle down now..."

Rita turned. "Hey, Charlene." By then everyone in the place seemed to be staring.

"What's that you got there?" demanded Old Tony Dellazola from his usual seat at the counter, three stools up from the door.

Charlene put on her widest, friendliest, happiest smile. "This is my niece, Sissy's little girl. Her name is Mia Scarlett and she's going to be staying with me for a while."

Did it work? Charlene asked herself that night, as she was putting the baby to bed in a nest of pillows. Had her bold move of waltzing into the diner and introducing Mia right up front like that thrown a wet blanket on the gossip mill?

She wished.

Uh-uh. It *had,* however, let them all know that Mia's "visit" was Charlene's story and she planned on sticking to it; that was all she was saying on the subject and they might as well get used to it.

But just because it was all that Charlene was saying, didn't mean everyone else would keep their big mouths shut. In the Flat, people talked. About each other. A lot. If you lived there, you had to learn to accept gossip as a given.

And some people were simply more interesting

as grist for the gossip mill than others. Troublemakers and victims of terrible tragedies topped the list of the gossipworthy.

Sissy and Charlene's parents had died in a car accident when Sissy was only nine. She'd been sent away to live with an aunt and uncle in San Diego, though Charlene had sold the family home to finance her failed suit to get custody of her sister. That was the tragedy part. And when Sissy returned to town last year, she'd been nothing but trouble. She was a gossipmonger's dream. Since she'd vanished last summer—no doubt with the contents of Brand's petty cash drawer in her pocket—the talk about her had never died down.

It didn't take a genius or a psychic to know what people would be saying. Charlene could just hear them...

"Sissy has a *baby?*"

"A baby poor Charlene never so much as mentioned until today, when she shows up at the diner with the sweet little thing in her arms..."

"Isn't that just like that crazy girl, to drop off her baby with Charlene out of nowhere like that?"

"You're right. Just like her."

"And I can't help but wonder, where has Sissy got off to now?"

"Yes. And the big question, the most important question, is who might that little one's father be...?"

Enough, Charlene chided herself. No good would

come from obsessing over all the hurtful things that people might say.

She needed to take action. She needed to find her sister. But how?

Charlene got out her address book. She had two San Diego phone numbers her sister had given her way back when Sissy was in junior high. Charlene dialed the first one, for a girl name Mindy: no longer in service.

The second was for a Randee Quail. A woman picked up after it rang three times. Maureen Quail, Randee's mother. She remembered Sissy, vaguely, but said she thought that Randee and Sissy had drifted apart in high school. Randee was a freshman at UCLA now. Maureen gave Charlene her cell number.

Charlene reached Randee on the first try. She said she hadn't spoken to Sissy since her sophomore year in high school and had no idea where she might be now.

Next, Charlene looked through the junk drawer in the kitchen and every nook and cranny of her desk in the living room. She found two phone numbers scrawled on sticky notes, no names attached, and she was feeling just desperate enough to try them both.

The first was a chimney-cleaning company. A machine greeted her and told her to leave a message. She didn't.

When she dialed the second number, a man answered. "This is Bob Thewlis."

"Uh. Hi. I'm Charlene Cooper and I wonder if—"

"Charlene. Yeah. At the diner up in New Bethlehem Flat. Well. Gave you my number how many months ago…?"

"Oh." She vaguely remembered—or she thought she did. Now and then a guy would ask for her number. She'd always tell them, *Why don't you give me yours?* "Well. Hi, Bob…"

He chuckled. "I thought you'd never call. Because you didn't."

"I'm sorry, I—"

Bob reminded her that he lived in Nevada City and he asked her if she'd like to have dinner Friday night. She almost said yes, just because she was so embarrassed to have called him and not even known who he was.

But then Mia started crying from her makeshift bed of pillows. Charlene apologized and said she couldn't and explained that she was trying to reach someone and had found his number on a sticky note…

"Bye, Charlene," he said, and hung up before she was through making excuses for her bizarre behavior.

She changed Mia's diaper and then sat in the rocker in the living room with her for a while, thinking bleak thoughts.

Not only had she totally misplaced her own sister, she also never had a date. Not lately, anyway. She *used* to date. She'd go out now and then when some guy would ask her.

But somehow, it just never went anywhere with anyone. A couple of dates and they'd stop calling— or she'd make excuses when they asked her out again.

There was just never a...fit. There was never that excitement, that special thing that happened when you met a guy who was the *right* guy. There was never the thrill she'd known all those years ago.

With Brand.

By Sunday afternoon Brand wanted to shoot someone. Or better yet, punch somebody's lights out.

Shooting and brawling did not fit the image he'd so carefully cultivated over the years. But too damn bad. A man—even a levelheaded man—can only be pushed so far before he had to start pushing back.

He'd picked up his uncle Clovis—who was also the senior and soon-to-be fully retired partner in their two-man firm—at five that morning. They went down to play golf in Grass Valley. Brand wasn't a great lover of golf. But it pleased his uncle if he played with him now and then.

The drive down to the golf course, on a twisting mountain highway, took over an hour. Usually that drive was a quiet one. It was early in the morning, and Clovis liked to sip the coffee he brought with him in a big red Thermos and watch the sun rise.

But that day, Uncle Clovis had plenty to say.

The way Clovis had heard it, Old Tony Dellazola had seen Charlene Cooper headed out of town—going east, in the direction of Brand's house, as a matter of fact—at a little before seven Saturday morning. Old Tony claimed he'd seen a baby seat strapped in the back of that silver-gray wagon of hers.

And then, at about seven twenty-five, Charlene had been spotted again, this time by Emmy Ralens and Redonda Beals, coming out of Brand's driveway and turning onto Riverside Road. Not ten minutes later, she'd shown up at the diner carrying a baby she claimed was her sister's.

"So *did* Charlene pay you a visit yesterday morning?" Brand's Uncle Clovis asked.

"Yeah. She did."

"I thought the two of you never spoke."

"As a rule, we don't."

Clovis waited—for Brand to offer some sort of explanation. But Brand had no plans to do any such thing. They rolled down into the heart of one canyon across a bridge and then began climbing again.

"You know," said Clovis. "Daisy and I always think of you as the son we never had."

"And I consider you like a dad, Uncle Clovis."

"If you got a problem, I want you to feel you can come to me, that we can work it out together."

"Thanks, Uncle Clovis. I appreciate that."

"So, then?"

"There's nothing. Believe me."

"You don't want to talk about it?"

"No. I don't."

For the rest of the ride, Clovis was blessedly quiet.

At the golf course, they teed off and played three holes before, at the fourth tee, Clovis remarked, "Charlene's story is that the baby's here for a visit."

"Yeah," said Brand. "That's what I understand."

"Kinda strange. I mean, that is a very young baby to be without her mother. And nobody's seen Sissy. That's odd, don't you think? Hard to get into the Flat without *somebody* noticing."

Brand handed his uncle his favorite driver. "Here you go. And don't worry, okay? Tell Aunt Daisy that everything's fine. Charlene's taking care of her niece for a while. No matter what wild stories folks like to make up, that's all that's happening."

Don't worry.

Brand wished he could take his own damn advice.

The stuff Clovis had told him ate at him. He knew people were talking, putting two and two together, deciding that there was only one reason Charlene would take her sister's new baby and go knocking on Brand's door.

If they weren't already saying that Brand had to be the baby's dad, they soon would be. Before you knew it, they'd be comparing him to his own bad dad, who'd managed to impregnate any number of gullible women in his long and disturbing life as a bona fide sociopath. Oh, yeah. They'd all be babbling on about how the apple never fell far from the tree and like father, like son....

Worst of all, he couldn't stop thinking about Charlene.

Couldn't stop worrying about her, wondering how she was holding up, what with not knowing where Sissy was and having to keep a brave face on things while she ran her business *and* took care of a new baby on her own.

His mother called at six-thirty that night from the B&B she'd been running since before Brand was born. She would have served her guests afternoon tea by then. Dinner was for herself—and maybe her boyfriend, Alyosha Panopopoulis, a widower she'd been dating for over a year. Bowie and Buck both lived out of town now, but sometimes she'd invite Brett to bring Angie and the baby over. And sometimes she'd call Brand.

Chastity said, "I've got that chicken broccoli casserole you like in the oven."

"The one with the almonds and water chestnuts?"

"That's it."

"I'll be there. Ten minutes."

"I'll set you a place."

* * *

The best thing about Brand's mom was how she never butted into her son's business—well, almost never. Now and then one of them would really tee her off. Then she'd let them know in no uncertain terms what they'd done wrong and what they'd better do about it. But such times were rare.

Usually, a man could sit at her kitchen table in the back of the B&B and enjoy her cooking and her calm, easygoing ways, and never be asked to come up with an answer to an uncomfortable question.

And so it was that night. Chastity had a whiskey and soda waiting for him. He sat at the table and sipped it as she cut up a green salad and took homemade bread from the oven to cool.

They talked of ordinary stuff: how his practice was picking up, now he'd pretty much taken over from Clovis who'd only been in the office part-time for the past five or six years. Brand was attracting clients from all over the county, as well as several from down in Nevada City and Grass Valley.

Chastity said she was thinking of redoing a couple of the guest rooms upstairs. "I talked to Glory today," she added.

Glory Dellazola and Bowie, Brand's youngest brother, had been in love—and probably still were. Glory had gotten pregnant. Bowie had wanted to marry her. But Bowie was big trouble and she wouldn't have him. In the end Glory had taken their baby and moved to New York to work for Brand's oldest brother, Buck, and his wife, B.J. Glory was nanny for Buck's son, Joseph James.

No one knew where Bowie was. He'd left town without telling anyone where he was going.

"So how's Glory doing?" Brand sipped his drink.

"Just fine," said Chastity. "She's taking those online classes the way she planned, getting herself a degree."

"That's good."

Chastity put the casserole on the table, along with the bread and the salad. And then she took her chair, smoothed her napkin on her lap and said a short grace, the way she always liked to do.

Brand bent his head, too.

His mother said, "Amen."

Brand glanced up and met her eyes across the table. And suddenly it seemed the best thing, just to say what was on his mind.

"Ma?"

"Hmm?"

"I want another chance with Charlene."

"Well, of course you do," said Chastity. She picked up the serving spoon. "Pass me your plate."

Chapter Four

"I think I need another drink," Brand said.

Chastity spooned up the steaming casserole. "Help yourself."

So he carried his glass to the refrigerator and got some more ice. She'd left the Crown Royal on the counter. He splashed in two fingers and then added club soda.

Thus fortified, he took his seat again. "Smells great." He sipped the drink.

"Dig in."

They ate in silence for a while. She didn't push him. It wasn't her way.

She was slicing more bread off the loaf when she

sensed he was watching her. She set down the bread knife. "Okay. Out with it."

"No matter what people are saying, I'm not the father of Sissy's baby."

She made a snorting sound. "Well, of course you're not."

He sipped his drink again. "You're sounding pretty damn sure about every little thing this evening."

"I know what's what, thank you very much. I know my own son."

He tipped his glass to her in a salute. "Meaning?"

"Meaning, how can you be the father of that baby when you never laid a hand on that poor, confused Sissy Cooper? You could never do a thing like that. Not only because you wouldn't take advantage of a mixed-up kid, but also because you are and always have been in love with her sister."

"I didn't say I was in love with Charlene."

"See now, that's what comes of bein' overly careful. You can't even admit what's in your own heart."

"And I'm not necessarily talking about marriage."

"Do you see me putting words in your mouth?"

"I've never thought I'd make a good husband."

"No kidding."

He grumbled, "And who knows if she'll ever even give me any kind of break. She never has until now. Plus, it's not only folks in town whispering that I'm the baby's father. Sissy claims I am."

Chastity clucked her tongue. "That girl. Always stirring the pot. And where *is* Sissy, anyway?"

He glanced toward the door to the hallway, just to make sure it was shut. "Nothing I say leaves this room."

"This is family business. I will not say a word to anyone."

"Charlene has no idea where Sissy is."

"But the two of them must have talked, when Sissy arrived with the baby…."

"No."

"But…"

"Charlene woke up yesterday morning and found the baby on her couch. There was a note from Sissy saying how she needs a break from being a mother— and by the way, *I'm* the dad. Charlene came flying over to my place and demanded that I take responsibility."

"And you told her you aren't the dad."

"I told her."

"Did she believe you?"

"I don't think she knows *what* to believe."

"It'll be no easy task, gettin' back in her good graces."

"Gee, Ma. Tell me something I don't already know."

The diner was closed Sundays.

A good thing, too. Charlene had needed a free day for a trip to Grass Valley, where she stocked up on formula and diapers, bought a crib and a changing table, baby clothes, blankets and the hundred other things a person needed with an infant in the house.

At home again in the afternoon, she managed to assemble the crib and the changing table. She put them both in the guest room off the kitchen, washed all of Mia's new bedding and clothing and put them away.

With Mia's room set up, she'd started thinking she was really going to need day care. She called Gracie Dellazola, the wife of one of Old Tony's great-grandsons—and the sister-in-law of Glory, who'd had a baby by one of Brand's brothers the year before. Gracie had a two-year-old son and she babysat the kids of a couple of Charlene's customers.

"Of course I can take her." Gracie quoted an hourly rate and said she could watch the baby from Monday through Friday. "But unless you're really stuck, I can't do Saturdays. I like to save the weekends for the family."

"I understand. I'll figure something out for Saturdays." She might have to bring another waitress in to open up that one day. It was doable. "If you could keep her from quarter of six until two or so, Monday through Friday? Is that too much?"

"No problem."

"I'm figuring I can drop in and take her off your hands, now and then, when things aren't too crazy at the diner."

"Sure—and listen, if you need anything…"

My sister. I need my sister to come home, I need to know she's okay, not in any kind of trouble. I need to keep this baby safe…. "Thanks. I'm fine."

"Sometimes," Gracie said softly, "a woman needs a friend."

Charlene felt the moisture pool in her eyes. She cleared her throat. "See, that's what I love about livin' in the Flat. Neighbors like you, Gracie. You make it all worthwhile."

"I'm here. That's all. I can listen. And I know how to keep my mouth shut."

"Thank you."

"Tomorrow morning, then?"

"We'll be there, Mia and me. With bells on."

And speaking of wonderful neighbors, Chastity Bravo called that evening at a little after eight. Charlene had always liked Chastity. She liked Brand's brothers, too—even Bowie, who'd been a hopeless drunk and general hell-raiser before he left town last year. Just because she couldn't tolerate Brand didn't mean she had anything against the rest of his family.

Chastity said, "I heard you were taking care of your sister's baby for a while, and I just wanted you to know if you need anyone to babysit now and then…"

"Gracie Dellazola said she could take her. But thanks so much, Chastity, for offering."

"I'm glad to. My schedule's pretty flexible, and the truth is I really enjoyed having a baby around." Glory and her baby had stayed with Chastity for a while right after the baby was born.

"Well, if there's a time Gracie can't take her, I'll be calling."

"See that you do."

Charlene said goodbye and felt better about things—at least for a while.

Her worrying about Sissy just wouldn't stop, though. Really, she was glad to have Mia, happy to take care of her for as long as Sissy needed her to.

But where was Sissy?

And was she okay?

She read Sissy's note over and over, looking for clues as to how she was doing and where she might have gone. The note gave her nothing, though—not when it came to Sissy's circumstances or her current location.

Monday and Tuesday Charlene got used to the idea of working her schedule around Mia. Both days she picked the baby up after the lunch rush and went home for a couple of hours, then she took Mia with her back to the diner until she closed up at five.

By Wednesday, she was feeling pretty good about the way it was working out. Mia seemed happy enough spending her mornings with Gracie and Baby Tony. Since she was such an easy baby, she was no trouble at the diner. And Gracie's sisters-in-law had a whole lot of baby stuff between them. They loaned Charlene a playpen for the diner and one for the house, a baby seat and a baby pack that hooked on in the front. Since she never took the baby to the diner when she actually had to work the tables, it was fine. She could have Mia in the office while she did her bookkeeping, or even sitting in her little seat out in the main part of the restaurant, if necessary.

If only she weren't so worried about Sissy, she'd be feeling pretty good about the way things were going.

Wednesday evening, when she and Mia got home from the diner, she did the thing she really *didn't* want to do.

She called her aunt Irma in San Diego and asked if Irma might know of a way that she could get in touch with Sissy.

Irma Foxmire hadn't changed. She was as self-righteous and judgmental as ever. In that tight, chilly voice of hers she said, "Well, Charlene. What can I say to you? Your uncle Larry and I haven't seen Sissy in over a year—not since before she came to stay with you. No, she has not called. I have no idea how to reach her. And *you* haven't called, either, as a matter of fact." Irma exhaled, a hard sigh of anger and impatience. "Is there some emergency we should know about?"

It was the moment to mention Mia. Charlene let that moment pass. As she'd told Brand, she wasn't giving Mia up to CPS. And she was afraid if Irma knew about the baby, the first thing the woman would do was to call them and have Mia taken away.

"Hello? Charlene? Are you still on this line?"

"I'm here, Aunt Irma."

"Answer my question, then. Please."

"No. There's no emergency." *Not that I know of, anyway.* "I'm just trying to get hold of my sister, that's all."

"She didn't even have the courtesy to leave you a phone number where you could reach her?"

"Aunt Irma—"

"Never mind. You don't need to tell me. I already know. And I must say, if she's gone, well, just think of it as good riddance to bad stuff. I certainly do. That girl was nothing but a heartache and an ongoing trial to Larry and me. We gave her everything. And look how she turned out."

"Aunt Irma. I'm asking you nicely to stop running Sissy down."

Irma wasn't listening. But then, she never did. "Just forget her. I'm telling you, Charlene. Forget her. It's the only way."

It was too much. "No, I will not forget her. She's my sister and I love her." *Temper, temper,* Charlene thought. *I am going to shut up now.* But she didn't. "And in case you don't remember, Sissy was a sweet, funny, loving little girl before you took her away to live with *you*."

Irma gasped. "I did what was right for her, at considerable cost to myself and my marriage. Your sister has messed up her own life, thank you very much. All I ever did was to feed and clothe her and try to bring her up right—and I don't wish to discuss this subject further."

"Hey. Fine by me." The line went dead. "Bitch," Charlene muttered to the dial tone. She hung up and glanced over at her niece, who was cooing happily at the butterfly mobile suspended above the playpen. "All right. I know what you're thinking. I should have been more reasonable. But that woman just makes my blood boil."

Mia made one of those noises that sounded like a giggle.

"Okay. I'm sorry I called her a bitch. I mean, she is one. But it's not nice to say so. And I hope when you get old enough to talk, you'll be a more forgiving person than your Aunt Charlene."

"Go-wahhhh…"

"My sentiments, exactly." The doorbell rang. "Terrific. What now?" She marched into her tiny foyer, flung the door wide—and found Brand waiting on the other side.

Chapter Five

He said, "Since Sunday, I've been trying to work up the nerve to come over here." He gazed at her hopefully. He seemed so sincere and he was so tall and broad-shouldered and handsome and...*capable* looking.

She could have hated him just for that alone. For looking like everything she wanted and needed in a man—when he wasn't. "Okay. I'll bite. Why in the world would you want to come over here?"

He stuck his hands in the pockets of his khaki slacks and lifted one fine, hard shoulder in a shrug. "It's not right you should have to take care of that baby on your own. Let me...help out."

Okay, now. That was a stunner. "Let you *what?*"

"I want to help out."

"What did I tell you about helping? I believe it was 'don't.'"

He frowned. "But you *need* help. You shouldn't have to do this on your own."

"So you're admitting it, then? Mia *is* yours."

"Charlene. How many times do I have to say it? I never slept with your sister, so that baby can't be mine."

There was no point in arguing with him. No point in even *talking* with him. "Brand. Go away. Just, please, leave me alone." She swung the door shut. But it wouldn't go. Because his foot was in it. She glared at him through the narrow space that remained between the door and the door frame. "Move your foot."

"Let me in."

She looked down at that foot of his and then back up at him. "I ought to call the sheriff on you."

Brand said nothing, though one golden-brown eyebrow sort of inched toward his hairline. And his foot? It stayed right where he'd put it a few seconds ago. Stuck firmly between her door and the door frame.

It was either start screaming at him—or let him in where she could yell at him in the privacy of her own home. "Fine," she said between clenched teeth.

She turned from him and marched into the living

room—past the playpen and around the coffee table. Brand came in behind her and quietly shut the door as she dropped to the sofa. She could see him in her side vision, though she refused to look directly at him. Instead she focused on Mia, who continued to make those happy little baby noises and stare up at the butterfly mobile as if it was the most fascinating thing she'd ever seen.

He came and stood above Charlene. She kept her gaze on the baby.

"You're not even going to look at me?"

She was not. "If you've got something to say, get it over with."

From the corner of her eye she could see his hands hanging at his sides. They tightened. And then he must have caught himself because they visibly relaxed.

Those hands…

Sometimes she could still remember the way they felt, touching her—and why, oh, why did she have to think about him touching her right now, when he was standing six inches away, waiting for her to give up and face him?

"I'm sorry," he said.

Surely she'd heard wrong. She raised her head and met his waiting eyes; though, only a second before, she'd promised herself she wouldn't. "What?"

"I said, I'm sorry for ten years ago. I shouldn't have walked away from you. I didn't know what the hell else to do. I was twenty years old and incapable of being the kind of man that you needed then. I knew I'd make one lousy husband. I was certain it would be a disaster—not only the marriage part but also trying to be an instant dad to a nine-year-old kid. I couldn't deal. So I broke it off."

She stared up at him. "You couldn't deal…"

"That's right. I was a coward and I ran. I left you to fight for your sister on your own."

"And now you want, what? My forgiveness? For me to tell you it's okay and I'm over it? Well, Brand, I know I *should* be over it. I should be…a bigger person than I am. But I'm not a bigger person and I'm not over it."

"I know you're not."

"I don't even want to talk about it."

"Fine."

She wanted to…oh, she didn't know what she wanted to do. But it included violence. And even blood. "Fine?" she demanded.

"That's what I said."

"No, Brand. It's not fine. It's not fine at all."

He kept his mouth shut, probably because he knew that whatever he said at that moment would only cause her to start shrieking. He stared down at her, waiting—for what, she had no idea.

The awful question, the one she couldn't stop asking herself—and him—rose in her mind again, *Had he slept with Sissy?*

Did she actually believe he could do such a low,

rotten thing? Beyond not being the kind of man she could count on, was he also a liar and a cheat, a guy who'd have sex with her own little sister and then deny that her sister's baby might be his…?

Her stomach was clenched so tight, she feared she might be sick. With a soft cry of misery and frustration, she put her head in her hands.

"Damn it, Charlene…"

She heard his voice above her, sounding every bit as miserable and frustrated as she was—and right then, she *knew*.

She was certain. He *couldn't* have done it, couldn't have slept with Sissy. He just…well, he *wouldn't,* that was all.

So while she would continue to judge him and find him guilty when it came to what had happened ten years ago, she had a gut-deep, undeniable surety that he was innocent of seducing Sissy. No matter how hard and loud she insisted otherwise, she *believed* him when he said he hadn't laid a hand on her sister.

Which meant either she was ten kinds of hopeless, gullible fool when it came to him—or Sissy had lied outright about something really important. Lied with breathtaking cruelty, choosing to accuse the one man she knew Charlene couldn't bear to deal with, the only man Charlene had ever loved….

It was all just too ugly.

Too sad.

Too wrong.

And Charlene was tired. She was bone-deep weary of being furious at Brand, of denying her real and growing anger at her sister.

She lowered her hands and folded them in her lap and drew her shoulders back. "All right," she said. "I've heard your apology. Are you finished?"

"No."

"What else?"

"I just want to help, that's all. Maybe make up a little for what I didn't do back then."

Surely this wasn't really happening. Brand in her house, saying he was sorry, telling her he wanted to make up for the past. "You want to help…"

"Yeah."

"You're kidding, right?"

"Never been more serious in my life."

He wanted to help….

Incredible.

As she cast about for an appropriate response to that one, she glanced Mia's way and saw that her niece had fallen asleep. Charlene shook her head. "Look at that."

Brand asked cautiously, "You mean the baby?"

"Yes. I mean the baby."

"She's…sleeping," he said, as hesitant as a bad student suddenly called upon to answer a question in class. "Right?"

"Yes. She's sleeping. All this drama, all this suffering. All this mess…and she just goes sweetly to sleep. I'm telling you, that baby has got life figured out."

Brand stood there above her, looking like he didn't know what to do with himself. "Charlene…"

Charlene put a finger to her lips. She went to the playpen and gathered the little angel into her arms. Mia sighed and snuggled in against her shoulder the way she always did, so trustingly. Charlene carried her—through the kitchen and into the spare bedroom. She put her in her crib, switched on the baby monitor and shut the bedroom door on her way out.

Back in the living room, Brand was just sitting there in the wing chair, waiting for her. Charlene went on into her own room and got the receiver for the baby monitor. She turned it on, took it back in the living room with her and reclaimed her seat on the sofa.

The pictures of her family in happier times taunted her from the wall across the room. She looked at Brand instead and asked, "You mean it? You want to help?"

"Any way I can."

"Then don't tell anyone about Sissy leaving Mia on my sofa."

"Charlene. I get the message. Nobody's hearing anything from me, I swear to you."

"All right, then." She scooted away from him to the far end of the sofa and leaned on the armrest. "I just talked to my aunt Irma." Now, why had she said that? He didn't need to know that….

"Irma," he repeated. Of course, he knew all about Irma. When Irma sued to get custody of Sissy, Brand was the first one Charlene had run to. She always told him everything in those days. He was her rock and her sounding board. She'd loved him more than anything or anyone else in the world—even her parents, even her little sister. Or she had until he dumped her flat when she asked him to marry her and help her fight to keep Sissy in town where she belonged....

But wait.

That was bitterness talking. And she really needed to get beyond the bitterness.

He asked, "Your aunt give you a hard time?"

"She always does. And I let my mouth get away from me and said a couple of things I maybe shouldn't have. But I didn't tell her about Mia. And she didn't mention the baby. I'd bet money she doesn't even know that Sissy was pregnant. I want to keep it that way."

He swore under his breath. "Charlene. Don't look at me like that. I'm not going to tell her. I don't even know the woman. I wouldn't recognize her if I passed her on the street."

"If she were ever to contact you—"

"Why would she do that?"

"Pure mean-spiritedness, maybe. Because someone might tell her about the baby and she knows your name, knows that you and I were together once.

I don't know. I never know why that woman does the things she does. But if she did get in touch with you, I would expect you to find a way *not* to talk to her— that is, if you want to help me so much."

"I do want to help you. And, okay. If your aunt Irma ever calls me, I'll be too busy to talk."

"Good."

"And, come on. She can't be *that* bad—can she?"

"You have no idea."

"Help me to understand."

Was this an actual conversation they were having? She should put a stop to it right now.

She didn't want him getting the idea that they were suddenly best pals or anything—but then she heard herself say, "You saw how Sissy was last year…." She waited for him to make some hurtful remark about her sister, but all he did was nod. So Charlene went on, "I know she had…issues to deal with, even before Aunt Irma took her away. I mean, our parents just…vanishing from her life like that, going over the cliff that night and never coming home again, that was hard on her. Real hard. The time she did stay with me after they were gone, she was too quiet, you know? And sad."

"That's only natural, though, isn't it?"

"I suppose. And I realize that Sissy probably would have had some problems as a teenager, anyway. But Irma's so controlling and she's always criticizing—and giving orders. Sometimes I think that woman lives for the chance to boss people around. And what do you know? Sissy's turned out hurt and bitter and totally resistant to any kind of authority."

"No kidding," he said, with a wry twist to his mouth. She gave him a scowl, just to make sure he didn't forget that she wasn't going to take him running Sissy down. He added, "I'm a little unclear as to why you called your aunt, if you knew all you'd get for your trouble was a bad time."

Resentment flared. She tamped it down. He'd said he would help her. And she was starting to think of another way he could do that—beyond keeping quiet about Mia and Sissy.

She said, "I told you that Sissy left me no clue how to reach her. I don't even know where to start looking for her."

"So you thought your aunt might give you a number?"

"I hoped. But I guess I should have known better. Last year she and Sissy had their…final blowup, I guess you could say. She found out Sissy hadn't been to class in over two months, that Sissy had even gone so far as to intercept letters and calls from the school to keep Irma from finding out. Irma got so mad, she ransacked Sissy's room looking for drugs."

"Did she find any?"

"On a need-to-know basis, you *don't*. The upshot

was that Irma kicked her out and told her never to come back."

"And your sister came to live with you. But that didn't work out, either, right?"

"She didn't even finish high school. It's just so damn…sad. Even *I* managed to get through my senior year."

"You were valedictorian, too," he said. He sounded almost proud.

She'd been tops in her class. A small class, admittedly. In the Flat, a graduating class of fifteen or twenty was the norm. But she'd had a 4.0 and she'd been offered a free ride to both Cal State Sacramento and U.C. Davis.

He must have known what she was thinking. "You turned down your scholarships."

She shrugged. Defiantly. "I've got no regrets— not about that, anyway. I like running my own business. And I always planned to come back home after college, anyway. And you know, now we're having this cozy little talk, I've been wanting to ask you…"

"Why do I feel the urge to duck about now?"

"What happened between you and Sissy last year? What made her run away? What made her break into your office and steal the petty cash?"

He looked at her dead-on, no wavering—because he had nothing to hide? Or because he wanted her to *believe* he had nothing to hide? "I don't know why she ran away. Why did Sissy do any of the things she's done? And we've got no proof she's the one who let herself into my office that night."

"You're hedging."

"No. I'm saying I don't know any more about the night she left than you do."

"That doesn't help."

"Sorry."

"But there *is* something else you can do for me— if you're really serious about this helping thing."

"Name it."

"I want you to help me find her, Brand."

Chapter Six

Brand did look away then—away and then back. "Let me get this clear. You have no idea where to reach her, no address, no phone number, no names of friends or relatives, besides the evil Irma."

"I have two phone numbers of girls she knew when she was in junior high. One's disconnected. I reached the other girl, but she said she hadn't seen Sissy in years."

"Okay, then. You've got two *useless* phone numbers."

"That's exactly what I've got, which is where you come in. You're a lawyer. Don't lawyers hire detectives now and then—you know, to get the goods on cheating husbands and stuff like that?"

"Occasionally I'll hire an investigator, yes."

"So hire one now. Someone to find my sister."

He studied her for a long moment. In the end he nodded. "All right. I'll see what I can do."

"Thanks," she said, and knew she didn't sound the least grateful. She stood. "And you know, I think we're done here, don't you?"

"If I say I don't think we're done at all, is that going to make any difference?"

"No."

He looked at her expectantly for a few seconds. When she didn't relent, he gave up and rose. She herded him toward the door and even opened it for him.

But he didn't just go out and leave it at that. Oh, no. "I was thinking…"

She had the most awful feeling that he was going to do something really scary—like ask her out to dinner or maybe a movie. "Look," she said. "Don't. Okay?"

One side of his mouth kicked up. "Don't think?"

He was altogether too charming and he always had been, with his fine, lean-but-buff body and gorgeous eyes and that sexy cleft in his chin. What was he after here, really? What did he hope to gain? Was this sudden desire to help her only about guilt over what had happened way back when?

She said, "I just want to make this clear, Brand. Other than not telling anyone how Mia got to my house, and finding me a good detective to track my sister down, I don't need any help. I truly don't. I'm managing just fine."

His gorgeous eyes gleamed. And he wore the nicest aftershave now. Back when they were kids, it was the dimestore kind. She used to like it just because he was wearing it.

But now…

This close—which was *too* close—she had to keep reminding herself not to take in a long, hungry breath through her nose, just suck in the scent of him, he smelled so good. Not only manly…

But pricey.

She took a step back, far enough that she couldn't smell him. "I'm serious. I'm managing. Gracie Dellazola is taking Mia when I have to work. And even your mother called and offered to watch her if I needed a break."

"Ma called? When?"

"Sunday night."

"Well, good. I hope you'll let her take the baby now and then." His smile widened a fraction, as if he had some secret he had no intention of sharing. "She likes babies."

Charlene felt defensive again. She did have to watch herself. It was one thing to try and learn a little forgiveness when it came to him, and another altogether to let him get too far under her skin. "Admit it. You don't even remember her name."

"Huh? It's Chastity."

"Not your mother. The baby. My sister's baby that you're just falling all over yourself to help me out with."

"Of course I remember. And what the hell pulled your chain all of a sudden? I thought—"

"See? There you go. Thinking again."

He stepped toward her. She moved back—and then realized she'd retreated. She held her ground when he took a second step, even though it brought him much too close again. She could see those amber lights in his eyes, raying out within the green. He said, "You should do something about that chip on your shoulder. It's gotta be damn heavy. Ever consider just putting it down?"

She wasn't letting him sidetrack her on this. "The baby. What's her name?"

He hesitated long enough that she was sure he couldn't know. And then he said, "Mia. Mia Scarlett Cooper."

So. Okay. He *did* know. She muttered, "Point for you."

"You never give an inch, do you?"

"I do not want to fight with you, Brand. I want to…get along. I truly do."

"Well. Glad to hear it."

"I want to…let bygones be bygones."

"Charlene. For that, you'll have to learn to forgive me."

"Listen. I'm working on it, okay? I'm doing the best I can."

He looked at her for an endless moment. And then finally, softly, he said, "Good night, Charlene."

She said nothing, only waited until he cleared her threshold so she could shut the door behind him.

He was back the next evening, at the same time. She answered the doorbell, found him standing there and reminded herself that she was not the least bit glad to see him.

"What?" she demanded.

He braced an arm on the door frame. She knew very well he was prepared to stick his boot in there if she tried to shut the door on him. He said, "Gee. It's good to see you again."

"What do you want?"

"I've got news."

She felt light-headed all of a sudden, and had to suck in a deep breath that just happened to be filled with the expensive, manly smell of him. "Sissy. You've found her…"

His teasing look faded. "No. I'm sorry, not that."

She clutched the edge of the door as her heart rate slowed toward normal again. "Then what?"

"Let me in. We'll talk."

"Brand."

"What is it with you, Charlene? You're the only

woman I've ever known who can make my name sound like a threat." He paused. They stared at each other. And then he said it again. "Let me in."

Her house faced an embankment, with tangled woods above. There was no one to see them if she simply refused him, if she insisted he tell her whatever he had to say right there and then, at her front door.

But she *was* trying to learn to get along with him. And if he wanted to come in for a few minutes, well, what could it hurt?

She stepped back and gestured him over the threshold.

"Why, thank you so much. I'd love to come in."

She shut the door behind him. "Why are you here?"

He cupped his hand to his ear, as if he hadn't quite heard her. "What's that? A beer. Well, now that is downright neighborly of you, Charlene. I would love a beer."

"A beer."

"Yeah."

"Oh, fine." She turned on her heel, headed for the fridge and that beer he just had to have.

He moved at a slower pace. She paused in the open arch to the kitchen and looked back to see him leaning over Mia's playpen.

"And how are you today, Miss Mia Scarlett?" He gave a nudge to the mobile and the butterflies danced. Mia squinted and screwed up her tiny mouth. "So good to see you again."

"Wa-doo," she said and made the giggling sound.

"I'm just fine. Thank you," he said. And then glanced up and saw Charlene watching him.

She felt foolish for staring—but she covered it well, she thought, by ducking from sight on her way to the refrigerator. She got a couple of beers, then two glasses from the freezer.

When she got to the table, he'd already plunked himself into a chair. She opened the bottles and poured out a glass, which she set, with the rest of the bottle, before him.

"Cold glasses," he said. "That's nice."

She took the chair opposite him and filled her own glass. "Okay. You're in my house. You have your beer. Now, what's up?"

"I hired an investigator to find Sissy."

She gulped the sip of beer she'd been drinking and set down the glass. "Oh. Well. That's good."

"He works out of Sacramento. Name's Bravo, as a matter of fact. Tanner Bravo."

That gave her pause. "You mean...another half brother?" Sometimes it seemed as if his notorious, now-deceased dad had had sex with half the women in America—had sex and married them and gotten them pregnant. With sons. So far, to Charlene's knowledge, no daughters had been found.

Blake Bravo was one for the record books. And

fast on the way to becoming the most…productive polygamist in history.

Brand said, "Yeah. Another half brother. And a half sister, too."

"He has a sister?"

"That's right. Her name's Kelly. I found Tanner eight months ago. In the Sacramento yellow pages. I've used him a few times since then. He's not only my brother, he's also really good at what he does."

She was tempted to ask him what a small-town lawyer had needed a Sacramento investigator for. But he probably couldn't tell her, anyway. What with client confidentiality and all that.

And then again, it wasn't likely he'd find many private investigators here in the Flat, population 860 on a busy day, now was it?

She drank more beer. "So then, what happens next?"

Brand took a business card from his shirt pocket and slid it across the table. "He'll be in touch with you. Tomorrow. You tell him whatever he needs to know."

She took the card. Dark Horse Investigations. Tanner Bravo. There was a phone number and a long list of available services, including missing persons. "What will he need to know?"

"Everything *you* know about your sister. Including those phone numbers you told me about."

"But one was disconnected and the other—"

He put up a hand. "Charlene. Just give him the numbers. And your aunt's address and phone number, too."

"Oh, God. He can't tell her anything about—"

"Stop," Brand said. "Listen." He waited, apparently to make sure she kept her mouth shut. When she said nothing more, he told her, "Tanner's job is to *get* information, not give it out. He won't tell your aunt a damn thing, I promise you. Also, you'll need to tell him anything that might be a starting place for him. What high school Sissy went to, the names of friends she might have mentioned in passing, places she talked about, anything you remember about who she knows and where she's been."

"I don't know a lot." She picked up her beer glass again—and then set it down without drinking from it. "Oh, Brand. I should know more about my own sister."

"It's okay." He said it kindly.

"Uh-uh. No. It's not. She...closed herself off from me over the years. And after a while, I kind of gave up, you know? Even when she came home last year...she was so hard to deal with. I didn't know where to start getting through to her. I didn't think I should push. So I didn't. And before I knew it, she was gone again...."

He reached across the table, brushed the back of her hand, and swiftly withdrew. She was grateful in spite of herself for that reassuring touch—as well as for fact that he didn't let it linger, didn't force her to pull away.

"You did what you could," he said.

"No."

"Damn it, Charlene. You did. You fought hard to keep her. It didn't work out. And you're doing everything you can for her right now."

"What am I doing for her? Nothing."

"You're taking care of her baby. That's something. That's a real big something."

"It's not enough."

"Well, it's all you *can* do, so it's going to have to be enough—that, and give Tanner whatever information you've got. You'll need to make a list of everything you remember about your sister. I mean her friends, her likes and dislikes, her recreational drug use."

That hit home. She plunked down her glass again. "Recreational drug use? I never said—"

"Write down everything, okay? No holding back. No thinking that you're protecting her by not telling Tanner all of it. Because holding back is only going to make it all the harder for him to find her. Do you understand?"

"I just don't want him to—"

"Charlene. Do you understand?"

"You keep interrupting me."

"Because I'm trying to get through to you. I'm trying to get you to realize what you need to do if you want a prayer of finding Sissy."

"All right. Okay. I realize. I do."

"Good." He poured the rest of the bottle into his glass. "Make that list tonight."

"I will. I said I would."

He drained the glass. "And how 'bout another beer?"

She made a face. "You sucked that one down fast enough."

"You're such a delightful hostess, you know that?"

"Why, thank you. I try." She got up and took another tall, cold one from the fridge, popped the cap off and set it before him.

He filled his own glass that time. "So. What's for dinner?"

"Uh-uh. No way—and this Tanner, how much does he charge?"

"I'll handle it."

"What does that mean?"

"He'll send me the bill."

"No. Wait. He's looking for *my* sister."

"I'm the one who hired him."

"Because I asked you to."

"Charlene."

"No, it's not right that you should—"

"Let me do this."

"I pay my own—"

"Please," he said.

She dropped into her chair and sipped her beer. A slow sip.

He spoke again. "You said you'd let me help, remember? This is a way I can help."

"I'm just not...comfortable, with you paying my bills, okay."

"I'm not paying your bills. I'm helping to find your sister. And it's dumb to waste a lot of time and energy arguing over this, anyway. We have plenty of other stuff we could be fighting about."

Well, he certainly had a point there. She heaved a big sigh. "All right. I'll let it go. For now. But I want to see his final bill, okay? I want to know how much this ends up costing."

He tipped his glass to her. "Final bill. Will do."

"Good." And though she refused to go so far as to offer him dinner, she should probably dig up something to go with the beer. "You want some pretzels?"

"I'd love some pretzels."

He stayed another hour. She should have shooed him out of there before then. But he actually volunteered to change Mia's diaper when she started fussing.

And that she just had to see.

He did pretty well, actually. Though he couldn't resist making man-type jokes about the whole process, jokes relating a loaded diaper to nuclear waste and the like.

Charlene laughed at his jokes. They were funny.

He'd always been funny. Along with charming. And much too good-looking for her peace of mind.

After he left, she cooked her solitary dinner and absolutely refused to dwell on how easy it would have been to thaw out a second pork chop. She fed and changed Mia and tucked her into her crib.

Then she spent a good hour and a half sitting in the rocker with a spiral notebook, chewing on the end of her pen, trying to get down everything she remembered about her sister's life that might help Tanner Bravo to find her.

There wasn't a lot. She'd known there wouldn't be, but somehow, looking at the two measly pages of notes she had, all she knew about her little sister's life since the age of nine...

That was a bad moment. A really sad, bad moment.

She booted up her computer and put the notes in there, so she could print them off for the detective whenever he called to talk to her. And when she went to bed, she put the notebook and pen on the nightstand next to the lamp, in case anything else occurred to her in the night.

Nothing did.

At four the next day Brand called her at the diner. "Tanner will be here in town at six," he said. No preamble. No *Hello, this is Brand.*

And no, she wasn't the least bit excited to hear from him. Again. For the third day in a row. "Okay," she replied, keeping her tone flat and completely noncommittal.

"Take the baby over to Ma's after you leave the diner. And meet us at the Nugget."

She cradled the phone in the crook of her shoulder as she made change for a customer who looked a little too interested, as if he was wondering who she might be talking to. And Old Tony Dellazola sat at the counter a few feet away. She cast him a surreptitious glance and he grinned at her.

Really, nobody needed to know it was Brand on the other end of the line.

"Let me call you back," she said, very sweetly, into the phone.

"I'm at the office."

"Fine. Five minutes." She hung up and handed the customer his $2.98, along with a bright "Thank you" and a blindingly cheerful smile. "Tammy," she said to the waitress behind the counter. "Keep an eye on the register."

"You bet."

Charlene picked up Mia in her bouncy seat and carried her to her office off the storeroom. She put the baby down and called him back. His receptionist/clerk/secretary, Rhonda, put her right through.

"Why do you need to be there?" she demanded when he came on the line.

"I'm helping, remember? Also, I'm buying dinner."

"We have not reached the point where we're deciding who's paying yet. We're not even to dinner. We're still back with why you even have to be there."

"Okay, okay. I don't need to be there. I *want* to be there. Tanner's my brother—and you could use a break from taking care of Mia." He kept after her. "Look. Take the baby to Ma's. Be at the Nugget at six. It'll be you, me and my long-lost half brother. We'll have a drink and some steaks. Then you and Tanner can go on over to your place and he'll talk to you about Sissy, get whatever leads you've got for him, ask you whatever questions he has for you. You can trust him absolutely. Tell him stuff you're uncomfortable talking about with me, that's fine. He won't repeat anything you say—not even to me."

"Wait. The three of us have dinner, then Tanner comes to my house. And *you* don't?"

"I want you to feel free to tell him everything you know. And I have a feeling there are some things you're not going to want to say in front of me."

"I don't see any reason to go out to dinner first."

He gave a grunt of impatience. "Tanner's coming up from the valley. It's a two-and-a-half-hour drive—if traffic is light, which it never is anymore. He deserves a decent dinner."

"Fine. You guys can have dinner. Then he can come to my place."

"Charlene," he said. That was all, just her name. And something about the *way* he said it made her feel kind of petty. Like she was making a big deal out of something really minor.

She gave in. "Oh, all right. The Nugget at six. He and I talk at my house, after. Without you."

"That's the plan."

"And *I'm* paying."

"Well, all right, Charlene. Have it your way."

Chapter Seven

Have it your way, he'd said. Right.

It was only as she hung up that she realized she'd just agreed to have dinner with him in a public place on a Friday night. By tomorrow morning it would be all over town that she and Brand were speaking again after ten years of stony silence.

And okay. More than speaking. They were going out together. Sort of. In the most general sense of the term.

"Goo-dah," said Mia from her bouncy chair in the middle of the big metal desk.

Charlene caught her sweet little foot in its mint-green romper and rubbed the sole gently. "Yeah, well. I guess if I'm letting him 'help,' everyone's bound to find out eventually. And I'm working on that whole forgiveness issue, you know? I think it's a big step in my personal growth, for me to agree to be seen in public with the guy."

In response to that, Mia burped.

Charlene called Chastity, just to confirm that Brand's mother really was expecting to watch Mia that evening.

"I'm lookin' forward to it," she said.

So Charlene dropped the baby off at five after five, went home and changed into a dress she'd bought months ago and never worn. She also primped a whole lot longer than was necessary—not that anyone ever needed to know that.

She headed back across town at five minutes of six.

Brand and a dark-haired guy, presumably Tanner, were sitting in one of the knotty-pine booths when she entered the Nugget. Brand, who faced the door, sent her a smile of greeting. The guy across from him looked around. Charlene could see a faint family resemblance. The dark-haired man was handsome in a brooding, intense kind of way. And he had that Bravo cleft in his chin.

Nadine Stout, headwaitress and co-owner of the Nugget, grabbed a menu from the stand by the door and led Charlene to the booth. Brand slid out and stood waiting as she approached, so she ended up sitting on the inside, beside him.

Both men already had drinks. She asked Nadine for a glass of white wine. The waitress trotted off to get it and Brand introduced her to his brother.

She shook Tanner's hand across the table. His grip was warm, dry and firm. She got an immediate sense of a man she could count on—though not of someone who would be all that easy to get to know.

Brand leaned close and said softly, "Nice dress." Now, see.

That was really kind of over the line, like something a guy would say on a real date. Which this was not, no matter what Nadine Stout—who was constantly hiding a knowing smile every time Charlene glanced her way—happened to think.

"Thank you," she replied, because it seemed the polite thing to say and this was certainly not the time or place to give the guy a hard time for paying her a compliment.

And all right. It did please her—that he'd noticed she was a little more dressed up than usual, that he looked at her with that admiring gleam in his eye.

Was she a sucker for this guy or what? Ten years after he turned his back on her when she needed him most—and here she was again, preening and feeling all giddy inside just because he admired her dress.

Nadine brought her wine and came back fifteen minutes later to take their order. Brand talked about how his practice was doing, and Tanner mentioned his mother and sister. He said he'd been born and raised in Sacramento, that he remembered very little about his father, who was rarely there. His mother'd had a hard time of it. She'd ended up putting both Tanner and his sister in foster care.

Brand caught her eye. "Sounds familiar, huh?" It had been the same for him and his brothers. The youngest, Bowie, had not so much as *seen* his father. Blake had gotten Chastity pregnant for the fourth time—and never returned to New Bethlehem Flat. But at least she'd managed to keep her boys at home.

Neither of the men mentioned Sissy. Or Mia. Charlene was relieved about that. Talk of her niece and her sister could wait until she and Brand's brother, the detective, were behind closed doors.

It was a little after seven when Nadine asked if they wanted dessert. Nobody did.

"*I'll* take the check," Charlene told the waitress, maybe a little more aggressively than necessary. Nadine whipped it off her pad and handed it over. Charlene paid up.

They'd arrived in separate vehicles, so Tanner said he'd follow her to her house.

Brand said, "Thanks for dinner," when they got out onto Main Street. He headed for his big, fancy Jeep in the lot by the post office.

Charlene watched him walk away and felt a little curl of wistfulness down inside—for what?

That the dinner they'd just shared might have

been a real date? That tomorrow, when tongues were wagging about how she and Brand were clearly getting back together, it would actually be true?

Never mind. Those were questions she just didn't need to ask herself. She turned for her own car, which waited in the lot by the town hall.

Tanner Bravo took a seat at her kitchen table and turned down her offer of coffee. Charlene went and got the printout of the list she'd made for him.

He took it and looked it over. Slowly. Charlene sat across from him, tension crawling along the muscles between her shoulder blades as she pressed her lips together—hard—to keep from babbling something nonsensical while the detective was trying to concentrate.

By the time he finally glanced up from the paper, she was practically vibrating in her chair.

He looked at her sideways. "You okay?"

She cleared her throat. "Um. Not really. I really want to find my sister."

"I'll do what I can." What? Did it seem that impossible, even to him—a guy who found missing people for a living? He felt in his pockets. "Got a pen?" She took one from the mug by the phone and handed it over. He scribbled himself a note on the list she'd given him. "A time frame question…"

"Sure. Anything…"

"How long was it between your aunt kicking your sister out and when she showed up here?"

"Well, I don't know. As long as it takes to get here from San Diego, I guess. It seemed to me like she came straight here. I don't know why I think that, but I do…"

"Does she have a car?"

"No—well, maybe she has one now. I wouldn't know about that. But last year she didn't. She'd *had* one, until about six months before she came to stay with me."

Tanner said nothing. He simply waited for her to explain.

She said, "Sissy got speeding tickets. And she got in three minor wrecks. Finally she had her license suspended. Our aunt took the keys away from her. The car ended up impounded. It was all a big mess."

"How did she get here, then, without a car?"

Charlene blew out a hard breath. "She hitchhiked. I hated that she did that. It's dangerous. But she always claimed that she could protect herself and that nobody had better mess with her."

"Why did your aunt kick her out?"

"Um. Sissy said it was for cutting school…."

Brand's brother looked at her as if he knew there was more to it.

So she told him what she hadn't been willing to admit to Brand. "And because Aunt Irma found, um, marijuana in her room." She watched as he scribbled himself another note and had to ask, "Why does it matter, how she got here, how long it took her, why my aunt kicked her out?"

He shrugged. "Possible clues to her whereabouts now. She might return to anywhere she's been before. And as for the issues between her and your aunt, well, that's background, and the more I know about her background, the more effective I'll be at looking for her."

What he said made total sense. And Charlene felt guilty for challenging him. "I'm sorry. I guess I'm not very helpful. I just don't know enough—" No matter how many times she admitted it, it still hurt like hell to have to say it.

"You're doing fine," Tanner said. He asked, "During the weeks she stayed with you, any friends of hers come to visit her?"

"No."

"What about phone calls from friends—or *to* them, to anyone from out of town?"

Charlene sat up straighter as hope dawned. "You're right. There were calls I never made. On my phone bill, after Sissy ran away. To and from San Francisco. And San Diego—and some other area code I didn't recognize. I called the numbers when I first got the bill, thinking maybe I'd find out where Sissy was. I got a couple of answering machines and left messages, but no one called me back. Two actually picked up. One was a guy. He told me I had a wrong number and hung up before I could say anything else. And one was a woman who swore she didn't know anybody named Sissy."

"You still have that bill?"

"I do, I think. It'll take me a few minutes to find it." She started to rise.

"Hold on," he said, and took a business card—same as the one Brand had given her the night before—from an inside pocket of his jacket. He wrote on the back of it. "Here's my fax number. Send me a copy of that bill tomorrow, if possible."

"Yes. I will."

"And can you tell me the dates your sister was here in town?"

Those dates just happened to be burned into her brain. "Five weeks. From Sunday, the twenty-second of May until sometime Sunday night the twenty-seventh of June, or possibly very early Monday morning, the twenty-eighth. She…ran off in the middle of the night. I woke up the next morning and she was gone and so were all her things."

He did more scribbling. She waited. Finally he said, "When did your sister become pregnant?"

"I can't say for sure. But most likely, it was last year, during the time she stayed here in town—I mean, unless Mia was born early, or Sissy lied about the baby's birthday."

"Brand told me you found a letter pinned to the baby's blanket."

"That's right."

"I'd like to see it."

"It's…it's kind of falling apart. I've read it so much."

"I understand. I don't need the original. Just a fax is fine. You can send it to me tomorrow, but I wonder if maybe I could see the original now."

"Of course."

He didn't say anything more, only watched her, waiting. So she got up and got the note from the secret compartment at the bottom of her jewelry box. She carried it back to the kitchen and spread it out on the table.

"There," she said, "See? She writes that Mia was born on March fifteenth…"

"That's believable to you? Does the baby seem the right age?" When she nodded, he added, "And nine months before that would be mid-June, when Sissy was living here."

"Yes. And, um, as you can see, she claims that Brand is the father."

"I see that. Do you believe her?"

It was the first time she'd been asked the question by a more-or-less neutral party. She told the truth. "The more I think it over, no. I don't. I just don't."

Tanner nodded. "And are you certain the baby is actually your sister's child?"

The question shocked her to her core. So much so that she had to stifle a gasp. "Well, I never thought…I mean, it never occurred to me that Mia might not be Sissy's. Who else's could she be?"

"I wouldn't know. But it's possible, right? You never saw your sister pregnant. You seem to think your aunt doesn't even know that there *is* a baby. You had no idea your sister had even *been* pregnant, not until the baby appeared on your couch…"

"True. But…"

"But what?"

"No." She said it firmly. "I see where you're going, but you're wrong. I know—I'm absolutely certain—that that baby is my niece."

"I'm only trying to consider all the possibilities, you understand? To come at the information from every angle."

"I do understand. And I'm telling you I'm certain that baby is my sister's child."

"How do you *know,* Charlene?" He said it kindly—in the way that you talk to deluded people, to people who refuse to face the truth.

Charlene closed her eyes. And a sense of certainty settled over her. She knew Mia was Sissy's. And she told Tanner why.

"Because I was nine when my sister was born. I can still see her baby face. Except for that little dimple Mia's got in her chin, that face could be Mia's face. There's just no way she's not my sister's baby."

Tanner said nothing. The kitchen was silent.

She could hear the antique clock ticking in the other room.

After a moment Charlene opened her eyes and found him writing more notes on the paper she'd given him. "So. What else?"

"A current picture of your sister would help a lot."

Of course. She should have thought of that. "I have a couple of snapshots I took when she was here last year." She rose again and got him the pictures.

He took the best one—of Sissy sitting outside on the deck with her morning coffee, her spiked hair purple at the tips, lips painted black, the safety pins in her nose and ears and left eyebrow glinting in the sunlight. "I'll make a copy. You'll get it back."

"I'd appreciate that. I don't have a lot of pictures of her in the past few years."

He picked up the paper and stood. "I'll start with those phone numbers you'll fax me tomorrow, those and what you've given me here."

"When you talk to my aunt…" She didn't quite know how to ask the question.

But he already knew what she wanted—probably because Brand had warned him. "You're my client. If you don't want your aunt to know about Mia, she won't hear about her from me."

"Thank you."

He actually smiled then, a wry twist of his lips. "Don't thank me yet. I'll see what I can do."

She followed Tanner out into the gathering twilight. After he drove off down her driveway, she got in the wagon and went over to the Sierra Star to get Mia. That midnight-blue Grand Cherokee of Brand's was parked in front, gleaming under the streetlamp.

Should she have known?

And why did her idiot heart feel suddenly light as a moonbeam in her chest?

Dumb.

Dumb, dumb, dumb.

She was not, she reminded herself as she marched up the slate walk—not under *any* circumstances— going to allow him to talk her into letting him come on over to her place. That is, *if* he had something like that in mind.

Chastity answered her knock. "Come on in the kitchen."

Charlene opened her mouth to tell Brand's mom that she just couldn't stay. But Chastity had already turned to lead the way to the back of the house. It only seemed polite to fall in step behind her.

In the cozy, warm kitchen that smelled of something delicious and lemony, Alyosha, Chastity's boyfriend, sat at the table with Brand. A widower who'd retired to the Flat a few years back and kept busy as the local handyman, Alyosha beamed and nodded at Charlene and she nodded back.

Brand said, "Hey."

She looked at him and he smiled at her. Her already absurdly weightless heart lifted up and floated right out of her body.

Dumb, dumb, double-dumb.

Chastity gestured at the chair next to Brand's. "Mia's sound asleep in my room. Sit down. Have a cup of coffee and a slice of lemon bread before you take off."

She was going to say how she really had to go. But somehow, she found herself pulling out that chair and sitting down. "Lemon bread, huh? It smells amazing."

"Smells great, tastes even better," said Alyosha.

So she had a cup of coffee and a slice of the delicious warm-from-the-oven bread.

"How did your meeting go?" Chastity asked, and Charlene was instantly worried about how much Brand had told her.

She sent him a sideways glance, and he gave her an almost imperceptible shake of his head, which she took to mean he'd revealed nothing he shouldn't have. "Just fine," she told Chastity, "My meeting went just fine."

"Well, good," said Brand's mother with a nod.

Alyosha frowned as if he might be wondering what meeting they were talking about. But he didn't ask. Chastity offered him more lemon bread, and the handyman eagerly accepted.

Too soon Charlene's coffee cup was empty and

her plate, as well. There was just something about Chastity's kitchen, she thought. It was so comfortable and it always smelled so good....

Chastity offered more coffee and a second slice.

But Charlene was already on her feet and pushing in her chair. "It was wonderful, thanks. But Mia and I should get home."

So Brand's mother ducked into her bedroom and returned with the baby, who blinked owlishly in the kitchen light, yawned and sighed—and went right back to sleep. Chastity carefully handed her over. Charlene settled the warm bundle on her shoulder and reached for the diaper bag, which Brand grabbed first.

"I'll carry this for you."

Charlene probably should have argued that she could handle the bag herself, no problem. But why make a big deal out of such a small thing?

She thanked Chastity.

"Anytime. I mean that." Chastity nodded at Brand. "You'll see her out?"

"Be happy to."

Out on the porch in the cool spring darkness, Charlene extended her hand. "I can take that now."

His white teeth flashed as he stepped out of reach. "No way. I give you this bag, it's good night, Brand."

She rubbed Mia's back. "Well, it *is* good night."

He dangled the bag by a finger—just far enough

away that she'd miss if she grabbed for it. "No way. I have to hear all about how it went with Tanner"

"There's nothing to tell."

He pretended to look pitiful. "Charlene. Come on...."

She didn't buy his act for a second. But then there was that other problem she had....

The one that involved her silly heart, which was beating too fast with excitement. With something that could only be called anticipation.

She was *so* losing all perspective here.

Her sister was missing, could be in just about any awful trouble imaginable. Any day now, her wicked Aunt Irma might find out about Mia and sic CPS on her.

And then there was the still-unresolved paternity question—and no, Charlene didn't believe it was Brand.

But still. It somehow seemed all wrong to get breathlessly excited over the guy her sister had accused of being the father of her baby.

And what about the original problem. The one of ten years ago. To learn to forgive was one thing.

To want to try again...

Uh-uh. Bad, bad idea. The pinnacle, the absolute summit of dumb.

And she *didn't*. Oh, no. She sincerely did not want to try again with this man.

And yet somehow, all her silly heart cared about

right then was that he was there, on Chastity's porch, in the dark, beside her, grinning and dangling the diaper bag a few feet away.

All her heart wanted was to stay there—or anywhere, as long as Brand was there with her.

Dumb.

Oh, yeah.

Dumb-de-dumb-dumb.

She needed to just say no.

But what she said was, "All right. My house. But only for a few minutes."

His grin widened as he swung the diaper bag back over his shoulder. "Let's go."

Chapter Eight

A kiss, Brand was thinking.

A man needed goals, and he had one for the evening: a kiss from Charlene.

Yeah, it had only been two nights ago that she agreed to let him help her, to try and learn to forgive him. Maybe, to some, two nights might seem as if he was rushing things a little.

Brand knew better. Two nights wasn't rushing. Two nights was too long. It was an eternity.

Especially considering all the lonely years of denial that had gone before. A decade of telling himself he'd done the right thing by walking away from her.

A decade of pretending he was happy without

her, a decade of reminding himself how it didn't matter that she hated him or that she snubbed him every chance she got.

Ten endless years of going out with…strangers.

There was no other word for them, for the women he'd dated after he broke it off with Charlene. They were nice, most of those women. Smart. Fun. And easy on the eyes.

But they weren't Charlene.

And so, to him, they'd always been strangers.

The good news, was all that was over now. He wasn't thinking marriage or anything. He wasn't going *that* far. He still didn't see himself as the marrying kind.

But he did want to be with her. A lot. He was more than ready to start making up for lost time.

And she was warming back up to him pretty fast, too—though you could bet she'd deny it in a heartbeat if he asked her outright. But Brand was an attorney, after all. And there's one thing all lawyers learn early: never ask a question unless you're sure of the answer.

Brand didn't intend to ask. He intended to *act*. And to do so the moment she gave him the slightest opening.

He realized it wouldn't be easy, getting a kiss out of Charlene. But hey. He'd known the goal would be a challenge when he set it.

"I'll just put Mia down," she said when she let him into her house.

He followed her to the tiny bedroom off the kitchen, dropping the diaper bag on a kitchen chair as he went by. She put the baby in the crib without turning on the lamp. Brand stood in the doorway and watched her, admiring the curve of her cheek and the sheen to her wavy blond hair when she bent over the crib and into the wedge of light spilling in from the kitchen behind him.

She put the baby down and covered her with a baby-size quilt decorated with yellow stars, stars he couldn't see all that well in the dim light.

But he knew they were there, crooked little stars sewn on by nine-year-old hands.

The quilt had been Sissy's once. Charlene had told him so years ago, when they were kids and so much in love. Way back when she used to tell him everything.

All her secrets.

All the little things that mattered to her, the details of her life. Like how her mom had made a baby quilt before Sissy was born and Charlene had been allowed to sew yellow stars on it.

Charlene had looked at him with stars in her *eyes* back then. He was her world then, he was everything to her.

Until he turned his back on her. Until he threw it all away.

She straightened from the crib, that blue gaze meeting his—and then skittering nervously away.

The baby monitor waited on the bureau. She switched it on. He moved aside, stepping back into the kitchen, as she approached the doorway.

"A beer?" she asked. "More coffee?"

"Naw. But, thanks." He moved the diaper bag to the floor and sat at the table. She sat, too—but left an empty chair between them.

Kissing her wasn't going to be any walk in the park, with her over there. And him over here.

He'd need to get closer.

Somehow.

She folded her slim hands on the tabletop. He calculated distances. It seemed a long way to reach, to put his hand on hers. Unless she reached out and met him halfway—which at that point, judging by the set to her jaw and the don't-you-even-try-it look in her eyes, wasn't real likely.

He remembered why he was here—other than the kiss, which he'd be getting to. Later. "So what happened with Tanner?"

"Just what you said would happen. He asked a lot of questions. I answered as best I could. He took one of the two pictures I have of Sissy from last year."

"He'll give it back."

"Yeah. That's what he told me—and he asked me if I was sure Mia was Sissy's."

That one kind of shocked him. "Well. Remember. He hasn't met Mia—or Sissy. He doesn't know how much Mia looks like her mother."

"Oh, God," Charlene said, and put her hand over her mouth. Above that hand, her eyes filled with tears.

What the...? He jumped to his feet and went to her. "Charlene. I'm sorry, I... What'd I say?"

She shook her head. A single sob escaped her.

"Hey. Come on...." He caught her hand and pulled her up. Amazingly, she didn't resist. She rose and she curled into him, burying her head against his shoulder. He stroked her silky hair, breathed in the sweet scent of her, as she muttered against his shirt, "It's only...you know it, too." She looked up then, damp eyes gleaming, a smile trembling on her soft mouth. "You know it. You just said so. You know she's Sissy's."

"Mia?" He gathered her closer. Damn. She felt so good. "Oh, hell, yes."

"Oh, Brand. I...I'm sure of it, too. But it's good, you know, that someone else agrees with me. There's so much I *don't* know, about my sister. There's *too* much I don't know. But it never crossed my mind until Tanner mentioned it, that Mia might not even be hers...." She had her face buried in his shoulder again.

He tipped her chin up with a finger so she would look at him. "Listen. Think. Even aside from the fact that Mia looks like Sissy, there's just no sense behind your sister leaving someone else's baby on your couch."

She sniffed. "But there's no sense to most of what Sissy does and—"

"Yeah." He put his thumb against her wonderful mouth to silence her. "There *is* sense to the rest of it. A twisted, sad kind of sense, but sense, nonetheless. Your sister's hardly a careful kind of person. So she slips up and gets pregnant. She decides to keep the baby—which really doesn't surprise me, somehow— and soon learns that taking care of a baby is way more than she's up for. But as luck would have it, she knows someone she can count on, someone who'll be sure to take real good care of the kid. You. But Sissy's got…issues with you, issues she's not up for facing any more than she's up for the responsibility of raising a baby. So she drops Mia off—and disappears."

"Leaving a note that says *you're* the father."

He touched her cheek. Because he couldn't help himself. Warm and smooth and soft. Just like he remembered it. "Your sister's got issues with me, too."

Blue eyes narrowed. "What issues?"

"You are such a suspicious woman." He stared down at that beautiful, wide mouth and wanted to take it.

But they were talking issues here. Never wise to kiss a woman when there were issues under discussion.

She asked again, "What issues?"

And he told her, since he could see she wouldn't

leave him alone until she had it out of him. "Your
sister resents me. She blames me, just like you do,
sees me as part of the reason she ended up with
mean old Aunt Irma at the tender age of nine."

"She told you that?"

He nodded. "The day I hired her. She came strut-
ting into my office wearing a skirt the size of a
postage stamp, those safety pins sticking out all over
her face, waving the Help Wanted ad I'd put in the
Sierra Times, announcing she needed a job and I'd
better give her one, that I *owed* her a job, that if it
wasn't for me turning my back on you, she'd have
grown up in town and ended up happy and well
adjusted with a high school diploma and scholarship
offers from all the best colleges."

"She *had* a job last year," Charlene grumbled.
"At the diner."

"Yeah. But she didn't *want* a job at the diner."

Charlene sighed. "So you're saying she still
resents you for what happened when she was nine…."

There was more, but it would only hurt her to hear
it. What he'd already told her was enough. "Imagine
that," he teased. "Someone carrying a grudge for all
that time."

"Oh, stop it." She shoved at his chest—but gently.
"I really am working on that."

"I know. And I'm glad. Real glad…" He waited,
holding his breath.

And it happened. She did it. She tipped that sweet

face closer to his of her own accord. "Oh, Brand. Just look at me."

He smiled down at her. "I am. And it's a pleasure."

Her mouth quivered at the corners as she tried not to smile back at him. "You know what I mean. Standing here with your arms around me. *Liking* it with your arms around me...."

"It's good that you like it. I like it, too."

"But I honestly wasn't going to do this."

"Do what?" As if he didn't already know.

"You know. Get...involved with you again. Rekindle the, er, flame...."

"So?"

"So. Look at us. This feels very...flamelike."

"Charlene."

"Humph."

"We all have a right to change our minds now and then." He ran his hand slowly down the slim curve of her back. She felt just right in his arms. She always had. Nice to know that *some* good things didn't change.

"I don't think so," she said without much conviction, her soft lips still tipped up, as if waiting for his kiss.

"I do."

"I don't...." But her actions gave the lie to her words. She tipped her mouth up higher still.

And he needed no more encouragement than that. He lowered his mouth until it touched hers.

Barely. Just…there.

Brushing.

Waiting.

Because he wasn't going to push her—at least, no more than he already had. He wanted her to be willing, wanted that more than anything.

More even than he wanted the kiss itself.

And then she sighed. And she slid her arms up to link around his neck. "Oh, Brand," she whispered, and rose up on tiptoe to seal the kiss tight.

Amazing.

Perfect.

Charlene's kiss. With a tiny, surrendering moan, she opened to him.

He gathered her tighter against him, groaning low in his throat as her soft breasts pressed his chest, slipping his tongue beyond her parted lips.

Tasting her, finding her as he remembered her in his secret dreams.

As he remembered—and more.

Oh, yeah. There was nothing—no one—like Charlene.

The taste of Charlene. So sweet. So good. So exactly right for him…

He was tempted.

More than tempted.

To carry it farther, to sweep her up into his arms and take her to bed. To start making up for all the lost years, right now, tonight.

But even he had to admit that might be rushing it. Reluctantly he lifted his head. After a moment she opened her eyes. Blue as the Sierra sky in summer, those eyes of hers.

He wanted to look in them forever.

She said, "I can't believe I did that."

And before he could formulate a suitable comeback, the doorbell rang.

"Oh, God," she said.

He pulled her closer, pressed his lips to her sweet-smelling hair. "Don't, all right?"

She tipped her head back, met his eyes. "Don't…?"

"Don't be afraid. Of what anyone's going to say. So what if they talk? They always will and there's no way to stop them."

"You're right," she said.

He stared at her. "Say that again."

"You're right. They'll be talkin' anyway, no matter what we do."

"That's the spirit."

"If we want to be…friends, well, that's our business, isn't it?"

He had a lot more than friendship in mind—and the kiss they'd just shared should have told her that. But, hey. If she wanted to call it friendship for now, fine with him. He'd met his goal for the evening.

Someday very soon he'd show her—in detail— why they were a hell of a lot more than just friends.

The doorbell rang again.

"Well," she said. "Guess I better get that."

Reluctant to let her go, but pleased with the progress he was making, he dropped his hands from around her waist and stepped out of the way. "Go for it."

She turned for the door.

From where he stood, he could watch her through the arch as she crossed the living room. He could even see into her small foyer area. He grinned to himself as she smoothed her skirt and then ran a hand down her hair, making sure everything was in order before she dealt with whoever had come knocking at eight-thirty at night.

She opened the door.

And she gasped. He heard the sound all the way from the kitchen.

"Aunt Irma," she cried. "What are you doing here?"

Chapter Nine

Anyone, Charlene was thinking as she gaped at her father's sister. *Anyone but Aunt Irma.*

And she had suitcases. Two of them. Big ones. They sat on the porch, one on either side of her.

"Surprise," Irma said grimly. Her slender face looked tired, and there were lines bracketing her mouth and raying out from her brown eyes. "I've come…for a visit."

Charlene said the first word that came to mind. The only word, actually. "No."

Irma blinked. "Excuse me?" She said it with surprising hesitancy. And she also appeared to be shaking. Was that possible? The uptight, always right Aunt Irma…trembling?

Charlene cleared her throat. "Is Larry with you?" Uncle Larry was a first-class jerk. He'd made a lot of money in real estate and he thought he knew everything. The man was so overbearing, he made Irma seem timid in comparison.

Irma blinked and smoothed her hair. "No, he's not. He…couldn't make it this time."

Well, that was something. Only one of them to get rid of. "Really, Aunt Irma. I had no idea you were coming. And besides, you and I are hardly speaking. A visit right now is just—" She cast about for words that would be tactful and final at once. None came to her. She finished weakly "—impossible."

By then Brand, who should have had sense enough to wait in the kitchen where Charlene had left him, was striding across the living room. She sent him a warning look, but that didn't stop him.

Irma put her hand to her chest. "Please. If I might just…come in. If I might just have a word or two." She blinked again as Brand filled the doorway. "Oh. Hello."

"Brand. Brand Bravo." He stuck out a hand.

Irma took it automatically and gave it a weak shake. "Brand?" She'd heard the name, of course. She glanced disbelievingly at Charlene.

Charlene groaned. "Yes. My high school sweetheart. Brand. We're…friends again. What of it?"

"Oh. Well. I meant no offense. Truly..." Irma tried to pull free of Brand's grip.

But he held on. "Great to meet you, Irma. Come on in."

Charlene elbowed him in the ribs and desperately shook her head. If Irma found out about Mia... "No. She can't. She really—"

"Of course she can." Brand gave a tug and Irma was over the threshold. Charlene stared in furious disbelief as he led her aunt to the living room sofa. "Here," he said. "Sit down."

"I...thank you." Irma lowered herself to the cushions.

"I'll just get your suitcases," he told her.

"Please." Irma nodded and shrugged out of her blue blazer, letting it fall to the sofa behind her. She stared at the playpen on the other side of the coffee table as if she feared she might be seeing things. She really didn't look right.

But whatever was wrong with Aunt Irma, Charlene's priority was Mia. And Irma was a danger to Mia. Irma had to go.

Charlene slid in front of Brand and shut the front door before he could go out there and get the suitcases. "I want to talk to you. Now." She craned around him and told Irma, "Back in a flash."

"Oh," said Irma, stirring from whatever weird trance had hold of her. "Certainly. No problem. Go right ahead."

Charlene grabbed Brand by the arm and hauled him into her bedroom. "What do you think you're doing?" she demanded in a hot whisper as soon as she had the door shut behind them.

"Charlene," he said, wearily. As if just saying her name was some kind of answer.

"If she stays here, she'll find out about Mia. And if she finds out about Mia—"

"What?"

She snorted. "You know what. She'll call CPS."

"No she won't."

"How do you know that? You don't know her like I do. You don't have a clue what she's capable of."

He pointed toward the door. "That woman out there is in some kind of trouble. She's also your aunt. You can't turn her away."

"I can. And I will."

He took her by the shoulders. She tried to shrug him off. But he wouldn't let go. "Listen. Think. She's here in town. The game is up."

"I don't know what you're talking about."

"If you send her away tonight, she'll only head for the motel or for the Sierra Star. By morning someone will have told her that Sissy had a baby— a baby who's staying with you."

"Oh, God. So…what? You think I should let her stay here and tell her…what?"

"Here's a wild idea for you. Tell her the truth."

"Oh, God."

"That poor woman out there is not going to be causing anyone any trouble."

"Oh, yes, she will. Just you wait. I don't know what's wrong with her tonight. But you don't know her. You don't know how she really is, how hard and heartless she can be."

"You're right. I don't. But I *am* a lawyer. I have…some clout with the Superior Court judge and with Social Services. I am promising you, Charlene. No one will take Mia away from you. I'm going to see to that. You have my word."

The crazy, impossible thing was she believed him. She actually believed him. She sagged against the bedroom door. "Oh, Brand. I'm so scared."

He gripped her shoulders tighter. "Don't be. Just tell her the truth—the basic truth."

"Meaning?"

"Tell her that Sissy's left Mia with you for a while."

"But she knows I don't know where Sissy is, that I was trying to reach her and didn't know where to look."

"Doesn't matter."

"But—"

"Just stick with the basic facts. You're taking care of your baby niece while Sissy's away. Don't elaborate."

"What if—"

"And don't borrow trouble."

"I'm not. It's only—"

"Wait."

"What?"

"Here's what we'll do. I'll take your aunt to Ma's."

"But a minute ago, you said—"

"Listen. It'll be fine. We'll visit first, just for a few minutes."

"Visit?"

"Yeah. Visit. Give her tea and a cookie—or a sandwich, whatever. Tell her about Mia. And then tell her you're putting her up at the Sierra Star because you only have the one extra bedroom and the baby's using it."

"Oh, Brand. I don't know…"

"I do. Now, come on. We can't leave the poor woman waiting out there all night. Let's go."

"I just don't know if we should—"

"Charlene. Let's go."

"All right. Fine. We'll do it your way." She yanked open the door and marched back out to the living room to find Irma waiting right where they'd left her, perched on the sofa, staring vacantly at the playpen, her hands folded tightly in her lap.

Charlene approached her as Brand brought the suitcases in and left them ready by the door. "Aunt Irma."

Irma shook her head as if to clear it. "Hmm? Yes?"

"Are you hungry? Would you like some coffee or…?"

"Tea. Hot tea. That would be so nice."

"I'll just get the water going."

Irma stood, leaving her blazer in a pile on the couch and trailed along after her into the kitchen. Charlene gestured at the table, and her aunt took a seat there. Brand came and leaned in the arch to the living room.

Charlene put the water on the stove. Then she turned to her aunt. "Aunt Irma. Are you…all right?"

"Oh, yes. I'm just fine. And I've been wanting to…apologize, for being so harsh with you. On the phone the other day. And…other times." She stared into the middle distance and put her hand to her throat again. "Yes. I have been. Harsh. With you. With your sister, above all. I have. And I know it."

Color me stunned, Charlene thought. More than stunned. Staggered. Astounded. Amazed.

Aunt Irma had just admitted that she had been harsh.

Brand was watching. And looking far too smug. Charlene rolled her eyes at him and opened the cupboard to get down the tea. She spooned Constant Comment into a tea ball and hooked the ball inside the blue-and-white pot that had once been her mother's.

Irma said, with surprising delicacy, "I notice there's a playpen in the living room. And I see a stroller…." She pointed to where the collapsed stroller leaned against the wall by the door to Mia's room.

Charlene gritted her teeth and came out with it. "That's right. Mia, Sissy's new baby, is staying with me for a while."

Irma blinked several times in rapid succession. Her hand seemed permanently attached to its position, flat against her chest. "Sissy…had a baby?"

Charlene kept it light. And bright. "Yes, she did. Mia Scarlett's her name. Born March 15."

"Oh. Oh, my…I…" At last Irma lowered her hand and folded it with the other on the tabletop. "Is the baby here now?"

"Yes."

"May I…see her?"

Brand spoke up then. "Tomorrow. Right now she's sound asleep."

"Oh," said Irma. "Asleep. Of course."

"In fact," he said. "It's a little crowded here at Charlene's lately."

"That's right," Charlene put in, more eagerly than was probably appropriate. "Only two bedrooms. Mine…and the baby's got the other."

Irma's hand inched upward yet again and settled on her throat. "Oh. I see."

"So we've got a plan," Brand said.

"You do?" Did Irma sound hopeful? Charlene thought so. Hopeful. And kind of lost, too….

Hopeful and *lost*. Two words she never would have thought of in connection with her self-righteous aunt.

"You're coming over to my mother's place,"

Brand said. "She's got a cozy B&B right here in town. You'll have a comfortable room all to yourself and you're in walking distance of Charlene's for as long you're staying here."

Charlene sent him a warning glare. It was one thing to put Aunt Irma up for the night—and another altogether to make the invitation open-ended. Brand pretended not to notice she was looking daggers at him.

She said, "I'll be over in the morning to join you for breakfast." Tomorrow was Saturday. Rita took the opening shift for her, now she had Mia to look after on weekends.

"You'll be over with my grandniece?" There it was again. That hopeful sadness. So strange. So…unsettling.

"Yes. Of course. I'll bring Mia."

"Oh, good," said Irma. She turned a wistful smile on Brand. "Thank you. Your mother's bed and breakfast sounds like just the thing."

So Charlene served the tea, along with a plate of the peanut butter cookies she'd baked the day before. Brand made small talk. Irma didn't say much, except that she was "rather tired," and was certain she'd be "more lively" in the morning.

More lively. What did that mean? Questions, demands and plenty of trouble?

By five of nine, Brand was herding Irma out the door.

The phone rang twenty minutes later. Charlene,

in bed with a novel open on her lap, snatched it up fast in hopes the sound wouldn't wake the baby.

It was Brand. "I have to ask. Are you sure that woman I took to my mother's is really your evil Aunt Irma?"

She laughed. Her heart was doing that happy-dance thing. She so had to watch herself. "I know. I can hardly believe it's her, either. I've been lying here in bed, trying to read and not succeeding, wondering what can be wrong with her."

"I'm sure she'll explain. Eventually."

"As long as she doesn't try to take Mia…"

"What did I tell you about that?"

"I know, I know. She's not taking Mia. You're going to see to it."

"That's right."

"And I have to admit, the Irma who knocked on my door tonight doesn't seem like any kind of threat at all. You think maybe it's cancer or some terminal disease? She's dying and suddenly she's realizing what an awful person she's always been?"

"Can't say…"

"Oh, God. I hope not. You would not believe how many times I've wished that woman dead. And if she really is dying—"

"Charlene."

"What?"

"Don't borrow trouble. And remember. Whatever she's going through, it is not your fault."

"Do me a favor," she said. "Another one. Please."

"Anything."

"Call Tanner. Tell him that my aunt's here in town. But I don't want him to talk to her. I just…I can't take that chance now. I don't want her stirred up. Tell him I really don't think she knows anything, anyway. And I want him to keep away from her, to just follow the other leads he's got."

"You are way too damn paranoid about this."

"Please."

"Hell. Okay. I'll call him."

"Thanks. For that. For…everything. For being here."

He was quiet for a moment. She held the phone in cradling hands and smiled at the far wall and felt ridiculously happy, just knowing he was on the other end of the line.

Finally he said, "I bet if anybody told you a week ago that you'd be on the phone with me tonight, thanking me for being here, you'd have told them they were out of their mind."

So true! She clutched the phone harder. "I shouldn't have kissed you. I know it."

His chuckle was low and way too sexy. "Yeah. You should have."

A warm, happy shiver went through her, a sensation as delicious as it was dangerous. Her breath snagged in her throat. She gulped. "This is all happening…really fast, don't you think?"

"No."

"But Brand—"

"No," he insisted. "It's damn well *not* happening too fast. As far as I'm concerned, it can't happen fast enough."

What was he telling her? His words made her dizzy. It wasn't wise to feel this way. She'd felt this way once before—with him—and gotten nothing but endless heartache as a result.

She had to…get a grip on herself. "But seriously—no. I mean, really. I don't know why I said that, about things happening too fast. Because, honestly, there is nothing happening. Not between us. It was only a kiss, that's all." He was quiet again. Too quiet. She couldn't even hear him breathing. "Brand? Are you still there?"

"I'm here."

"I just, well, I don't want you to get the wrong idea."

"Don't worry, I won't," he said, his voice flat, revealing nothing.

Should she clarify? Tell him right out loud that she was never going to fall in love with him—not again, that she just couldn't take that kind of chance a second time. The first time, after all, had been so much more than she could bear….

But he hadn't said he was in love with her, now, had he? And she refused to go jumping to conclusions about this.

She decided to play it positive. "I am…so

grateful, though. I want you to know that. You've been terrific the past few days. And the way you handled Aunt Irma, well, I couldn't have done that. I don't know how I would have gotten along without you tonight."

Another silence, then "Grateful's something. Grateful's a start. Good night, Charlene."

"Brand, wait…"

But he was gone. The dial tone droned in her ear.

Chapter Ten

The next morning at the B&B, Irma remained every bit as sweet and distracted as she'd been the night before. She held Mia, cradling her so tenderly, rocking her gently back and forth, and then beamed at Charlene. "She looks just like her mother, now, doesn't she?"

Charlene smiled right back at her and replied, "That's right, she does," wondering what in the world this nice lady had done with her evil aunt Irma.

"I hope she's all right—Sissy, I mean…" Irma spoke cautiously.

"She's just fine," Charlene replied, and prayed

that it might be true. Then she waited for her aunt to say something cruel.

Far from it. "Well, I'm so glad to hear that—you did reach her then, after you called the other day?"

Charlene lied baldly. Without remorse. "Yes, I did."

"Good."

Chastity appeared, as if on cue, and saved Charlene the trouble of having to come up with more lies about where Sissy might be and how she was getting along. Brand's mom served them frittatas and her famous Sierra Star muffins, and Charlene waited for Irma to ask about Sissy again. Or to start making demands, or at least to come up with a few unkind remarks.

She didn't. Irma remained the sweet stranger she'd been since last night. She said she'd decided to stay in town "for a while," that she needed "a break" and Chastity's "lovely little B&B" was just the thing for her right now.

"I'll visit with you and my grandniece. I'll…take it easy for a while." Irma stared out the window that faced Chastity's side yard, where the clematis twined the fence and the rhododendrons were just beginning to leaf out. "I'll take long walks, enjoy the rushing river and the quaint mountain scenery. This truly is a beautiful little town…."

Charlene had to restrain herself from gaping at her aunt in sheer disbelief.

After all, Irma had always hated the Flat. She'd blamed Charlene's mother for taking her precious only brother away "from civilization," off to "the sticks," where there were "deadly snakes and killer bears" and "nothing the least bit interesting ever happened."

"Aunt Irma," Charlene asked gingerly. "Are you...*sure* you're all right?"

Irma's smile quivered a little at the corners, but she tipped her chin high and drew her shoulders back proudly. "Oh, yes. I'm just fine." She looked down again at the baby in her arms. "And, oh, what an angel. A sweet, darling angel...."

Eventually Irma handed the baby back to Charlene, who had brought the bouncy seat. She put Mia in the seat, and the baby bounced contentedly as the grown-ups ate their breakfast—an excellent meal which Charlene found difficult to fully enjoy. If only she could stop flinching in anticipation of some grim demand or cruel dig each time her aunt spoke.

There were no digs. No demands. Not even any questions, really.

It was all just...very weird.

She wished Brand were there, though she knew she had no right to be wishing any such thing. She kept waiting for him to show up, swiveling her head toward the door every time she heard an unfamiliar sound, certain that it would be him.

But it never was.

Between flinching every time Irma glanced her way and constantly being on the lookout for Brand, Charlene was pretty much a nervous wreck by the time breakfast was over.

"How about a nice, long stroll in the mountain air?" Irma suggested as Charlene was getting ready to go.

"Oh, I really can't. I have to get over to the diner for a while, see how things are going there...."

"Well then, let me watch Mia for you until you're through at work."

"No. Thanks. I can manage, no problem...." Irma might seem like a whole new woman, but no way was Charlene trusting her alone with Mia. She still might call CPS—or head for San Diego and take the baby with her.

Irma leaned close and spoke softly, so none of the guests at the other tables would hear. "I know what you think of me. And I can't say I blame you. I only hope, over time, you'll come to see me differently."

Charlene had no idea what to say to that.

And Irma didn't seem to want her to say anything. She only put on that sad smile again and urged, "Go on, now. You and Mia see what's happening over at the diner. Thanks for stopping by and visiting."

"Come over to the house for dinner," Charlene heard herself offering before she could talk herself out of it. "Six o'clock?"

"I would love it. I'll be there."

* * *

Charlene used the fax machine in her office at the diner to send Tanner a copy of Sissy's note and of the phone bill for the month after Sissy's stay in town, with each of the numbers she couldn't account for clearly marked. Once it was sent, she put the original back in her purse. She would try the numbers again herself, as soon as she got the chance.

Out in front, everything was pretty much under control. She worked the register, bussed the counter and tables during the lunch rush. On a Saturday, lunch would usually go late. Things didn't start slowing down until around three, and since Mia wasn't fussing, Charlene stayed on without a break until closing at five.

At home, she changed into a white shirt and a fresh pair of jeans and prepared for dinner with Irma, who knocked on her door at six sharp. Her aunt stayed for three hours, during which she was pleasant and complimentary and held Mia every chance she got. Not a single harsh word crossed her lips and she didn't ask any questions, except about harmless things: "How's the diner doing?" and "This zucchini is so fresh. Do you get all your groceries right here in town?"

After the meal, Irma insisted on helping to clean up. "It's the least I can do after this delicious dinner you've prepared just for me...."

She complimented the house. "So charming. And

I love the picture window looking out on the deck." Ruefully she asked, "Do you miss that big white house you grew up in?"

Charlene thought, *You mean the one I sold to fight you for custody of Sissy?* But she didn't say that. It seemed too cruel a thing to say to this new, strangely sweet Irma. "Sometimes. But I love this little house and I still have my memories of the other one. And I can look at it anytime, just by crossing a bridge and walking down Jewel Street."

"I'm so sorry," Irma said, "that you had to sell that house. It's a regret of mine, that because of me you lost your family home. A regret among many, I must admit…."

Wow. Never in this lifetime had Charlene imagined she'd hear her aunt Irma admit to regrets. She said, "Well, it's gone now. And I'm fine right here."

The evening seemed almost as surreal as the breakfast at the B&B had been—surreal, but not quite so nerve-racking. Charlene was actually beginning to believe that her horrible aunt had really changed. She had to constantly remind herself to keep her guard up. Surely the bad Aunt Irma that Charlene had always known was bound to resurface. Nobody changed this much, this fast.

But it was the new, sweet, good-natured Irma who said good-night at nine.

Alone, with Mia asleep in her crib, Charlene considered getting out that old phone bill and making a

The Silhouette Reader Service™ — Here's How It Works:

Accepting your 2 free Silhouette Special Edition® larger print books and 2 free gifts places you under no obligation to buy anything. You may keep the books and gifts and return the shipping statement marked "cancel." If you do not cancel, about a month later we'll send you 6 additional Silhouette Special Edition larger print books and bill you just $4.74 each in the U.S. or $5.49 each in Canada, plus 25¢ shipping & handling per book and applicable taxes if any.* That's the complete price and — compared to cover prices of $5.50 each in the U.S. and $6.50 each in Canada — it's quite a bargain! You may cancel at any time, but if you choose to continue, every month we'll send you 6 more books, which you may either purchase at the discount price or return to us and cancel your subscription.

*Terms and prices subject to change without notice. Sales tax applicable in N.Y. Canadian residents will be charged applicable provincial taxes and GST. All orders subject to approval. Credit or debit balances in a customer's account(s) may be offset by any other outstanding balance owed by or to the customer. Please allow 4 to 6 weeks for delivery.

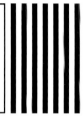

Would you like to read
Silhouette Special Edition® novels
with larger print?

**ACTUAL
TYPE SIZE!**

GET 2 FREE LARGER PRINT BOOKS!

Larger
Print
Editions

Silhouette Special Edition® novels are now available
in a larger print edition! These books are complete
and unabridged, but the type is larger, so it's easier
on your eyes.

YES! Please send me 2 FREE *Silhouette
Special Edition* novels in the larger print format
and 2 FREE mystery gifts! I understand I am
under no obligation to purchase any books,
as explained on the back of this card.

337 SDL ELZR   237 SDL EL3R

FIRST NAME	LAST NAME

ADDRESS

APT #	CITY

STATE/PROV.	ZIP/POSTAL CODE

Order online at:
www.eHarlequin.com

SLP-SE-05/07

few calls. But it was after nine and it seemed a little late to be calling up strangers to ask them if maybe they knew her missing sister.

Then again, maybe after nine was a good time to call. Catch them off guard, possibly reach a real person where last summer she'd only gotten recorded voices instructing her to leave a message.

She started dialing.

It was pretty much last summer all over again.

The rude guy somewhere in San Diego said the same thing he'd said back in July. "Wrong number." And the phone went dead.

The second and third San Diego numbers, she got automated answers—the kind you get on a cell phone—and left a message. The one with the area code she didn't recognize was no longer in service. She dialed the last number, the one in San Francisco. A young-sounding female voice answered on the third ring.

The girl said she didn't know any Sissy. "Hold on. I'll ask Dwayne. This is *his* phone." There was mumbling as she talked to someone on her end. Then she came back on. "Dwayne says no. He doesn't know any Sissy, either."

Charlene had the presence of mind to ask, "Who's this?"

"Zooey. Sorry, can't help ya." And she hung up.

Charlene tried not to be discouraged. She made notes about each of the calls and decided she'd try them all again later. Maybe someone new would answer, someone who could help her, someone who knew Sissy.

And next time she'd have a little speech planned. She'd tell them who she was, say she was looking after Sissy's baby and she really did need to get a hold of her sister. She'd ask for their help. Even really crabby people sometimes softened up when you asked them for help.

Still, it *was* discouraging. Why, any one of those people might know Sissy. And wouldn't it be just like her wild-child sister to warn them all not to tell Charlene anything?

Maybe Tanner would have better luck. He found people for a living, after all. He'd know what to say to them to get the information he sought.

She kicked off her shoes, fell back across the bed with a hard sigh—and thought of Brand.

Where was he right now? What was he doing?

Was he maybe out on a date with some nice, pretty woman? Some woman who didn't make a federal case of it just because he kissed her?

She sat up, reached for the phone again and punched up his number through her received calls. Funny about that thumb of hers. It started dialing, fast, before she could tell it to stop.

He picked up on the second ring. "Hello, Charlene." Of course he would know it was her. If not by instinct, by his caller ID.

"Okay," she grumbled. "So you're home."

"That's right." She could hear the reluctant smile in his voice.

"Tell me something…"

"Depends."

"On?"

"Ask the question. We'll see."

She went for it. "Have you got some nice, friendly woman over there at your house, someone who's waiting patiently for you to get off the phone and pay attention to her?"

"What do you care?"

Since he hadn't answered *her* question, she felt totally justified not answering his. Instead she said, "I was kind of thinking you'd show up at your mother's this morning for breakfast…."

"Miss me?"

"Okay, that's enough. You don't answer my question, you just ask one of your own. Is that like a lawyer thing?"

"No. And all right, Charlene. There's no woman here."

"You're alone?"

"Miss me?"

"Oh, damn it. Yes."

A tiny silence, then, "I'm alone."

"Oh," she said, and wasn't sure what to say next. So she was quiet. They were…quiet together. She listened to him breathe. How pathetic was that?

He spoke first. "You got something you want to say to me?"

She did. She just...couldn't quite frame the words.

He said, "Charlene?"

All she could manage was a sigh and a soft, formless, "Huh?"

"I'll come over."

It was the place where she was supposed to tell him no, the place where she was supposed to remind him that they were only friends and they would never be more, that she was learning to forgive him, but no way that meant he would end up in her bed or anything. And it most certainly didn't mean she would ever learn to love him again.

Too bad, at that moment, there was only one word in the entire world.

She said that word. "Yes."

Chapter Eleven

Six minutes later Charlene heard his soft knock.

Barefoot, every nerve in her body humming, she padded to the door, pulled it wide and there he was, dressed in cargoes, a white T-shirt and a battered pair of moccasins, looking just like the man she loved, the man she'd been waiting for, lonely for, hurting for…

For such a very long time.

She went into his arms without a word, without so much as a murmur of protest, without hesitation. Eagerly.

Hungrily.

She lifted her mouth, and his lips came down on hers, hard.

He took that first kiss. He claimed it, his tongue licking along the seam where her lips met. She surrendered and opened for him with a yearning cry. His arms banded tight around her as his tongue swept her mouth.

Her knees went to jelly. She was melting into him, her hands stroking his broad back, his narrow waist, the lovely, hard bumps of his spine.

Oh, he did feel so good.

He always had.

Though he was…different now.

Not taller, but…bigger. Broader than he'd been all those years and years ago. There was more depth in the wide shoulders, more muscle in the hard chest.

He lifted his mouth—just a fraction. She surged up to capture it again. He whispered, "Mia?"

"In bed." She speared her spread fingers up into his thick, golden hair and pulled his head down.

He didn't resist, but took her lips again with a guttural moan.

Fine with her.

Oh, yeah. No problem. He could have her lips. He could have everything, all of her.

For tonight, anyway. For now…

In the back of her mind alarm bells were ringing. But not all that loud. She knew very well she shouldn't be doing this.

But right then she just didn't care.

He walked her backward as he kissed her, into the

entryway. He caught the door with his foot and swung it shut, reaching behind him to turn the dead bolt.

She had hold of his shoulders. He felt so good, so warm, so hard. She pushed her hips up into him, to feel him wanting her, to show him how eager she was to be his.

Again.

After so long.

Too long.

An eternity.

The past, somehow was right there with them— and not the sad, awful past of betrayal and loss. Uh-uh. Before all that. Back when Sissy was the sweetest little sister around, when Sissy and Charlene had living parents who loved them, when this man in her arms was a gentle, sweet, loving boy.

A boy who adored her. A boy who said there was no one in the world like her, a boy who made her feel so naughty and so good, both at the same time.

Oh, the past…

The *good* past, the kind and loving past…

It was all around them now, pulsing inside her very heart. It was the blood in her veins, the sweet tears of happiness filling her eyes…

Brand caught her face in cradling hands. He lifted his lips from hers again, the twin fringes of his lashes parting, revealing those eyes she could never forget. His thumb brushed a stray tear from her cheek.

"You're crying. I didn't mean to make you cry. Not anymore. Never again…"

She laughed, a happy laugh, slightly husky with desire. And then she sniffed. "It's okay. Really. This is *good* crying."

He seemed unconvinced. "*Good* crying?"

"Just…kiss me, okay. Just kiss me and hold me and—"

He took it from there, covering her mouth again, wrapping his arms around her, lifting her feet off the ground. She twined her own arms around his neck, and he carried her that way, kissing her as he went, into her bedroom, where he let her slide slowly down his body until her feet touched the floor.

She sat on the edge of the bed and caught his hand, urging him to come down with her.

"Wait," he whispered, pulling free to whip his shirt off over his head and kick off his moccasins. His cargoes rode low. She could see the waistband of his red boxers.

She reached out. "Oh, let me help…"

He gave her the sweetest, most tender of smiles. "I like a woman who pitches in." One step and he was right in front of her. She took him by the sides of his hard waist and pulled him even closer, opening her thighs to accommodate him.

Glancing up, she found him looking down, his eyes low-lidded and gleaming, his mouth a little swollen from kissing her. She slipped the metal button from its hole and tugged his zipper down. It made a lovely, sizzling sort of sound. And then she took a handful of khaki in either hand and guided those cargoes over his lean hips. They dropped to the bedside rug.

He obligingly stepped free of them and made a move to climb onto the bed with her.

She put a hand—flat—on his hard, hot belly. "Not done yet."

He gave a low, oh-so-sexy chuckle. "Yes, ma'am."

Carefully she pulled the elastic waistband of the boxers out and over his erection. He took it from there, skimming them down and off.

She sat back on her hands and looked at him, standing there, totally naked in front of her.

Such a beautiful man, lean and muscled and tall. And fully aroused. Clearly wanting her....

So much the same as the boy she'd once loved.

And yet, so different.

The past washed over her again. She drowned in it, remembering...

That first night he came to her parents' house for dinner. She was fifteen and he was seventeen. He wore slacks that were too short for him, and he'd slicked his longish hair down to make it behave, but still a cowlick escaped and stuck straight up at the top of his head. He spoke so carefully and considerately to her mom and dad, wanting, she knew, to reassure them that, though he was a Bravo, he wasn't like his crazy oldest brother or his wild younger one.

Oh, yes. A special night, that one. The night she realized she loved him with all her hopeful young heart.

And a few months later…

The two of them, making love for the first time in the back seat of that old Chevy he used to drive, so awkward and eager, fogging those windows up, totally in love, swept away by young lust….

She'd never doubted they would get married. She'd known he was the one for her. He'd sworn he felt the same—that she was the girl he wanted to spend his life with. He used to tell her so, in the miracle of those first two years they were together, how he loved her, how there was no one but her in the whole world for him.

Then he graduated and went to junior college down in Rocklin and slowly, though she didn't want to admit it and even pretended it wasn't happening, she felt him pulling away—oh, he was still her guy, they went out every weekend. But something was…different.

It wasn't the same.

And then she lost her parents and knew she was losing her sister, too. She'd needed him so then. Needed him to stand beside her. To take her hand. To be her husband as they'd always said eventually he would be, to stand up before the judge and say that Sissy *would* have a two-parent home, a home better than the one Aunt Irma and Uncle Larry would provide, because it would be a home that was filled with love....

"I know that look. Damn it, Charlene."

She heard Brand's voice and realized she was staring blankly into the middle distance. Blinking to clear the sad memories away, she made herself meet his eyes. "This is insane. What are we doing?" When he only shook his head, she added, "I just...I don't know what I'm doing here. With you."

"The hell you don't." He bent over her, took her by the shoulders and pulled her to her feet. Then he framed her face in his hands again, the way he had a few moments ago, out in the entryway. "Think about it. You hated me for ten years."

"Exactly. That's what I mean...."

"*Hated* me, Charlene." His warm breath caressed her face and his scent surrounded her. She felt weak inside, at his touch, at his very nearness. He said it again. "Hated me. For a decade. You know what they say, don't you? The opposite of love isn't hate, it's indifference. Try and tell me you've *ever* been indifferent to me."

She marshaled a reply—no easy feat, with him so close and so...naked. "No, I've never been indifferent. But hatred isn't love. All your fancy arguments can't make it so."

"Damn it. Don't give me this crap. *You* called me tonight."

"You're right. But that doesn't mean I love you—or that I ever could love you. I just want that clear between us, okay? Not anymore, Brand. Never again...."

He closed his eyes, as if her words were arrows, wounding him. Then he brought his face that fraction closer. His lips hovered above hers and all she wanted was for him to kiss her again.

He whispered, "Okay. Clear on that. You don't love me. What about the rest of it?"

"The rest?"

"Tell me how you don't want me."

Okay, he had her there. At that moment, with him standing naked before her, staring right in her eyes...

Well, she just couldn't squeak out that big of a lie. She opened her mouth. All that came out was, "I..." She had no clue where to go from there.

And he refused to back off about it. "Just do it. Just say it. *I don't want you, Brand.* And I'll go."

She only shook her head as her yearning made a soft heat low in her belly, a lovely, lazy, melting sensation.

"Okay, then." His eyes said he understood perfectly what he did to her, what he made her feel. "You want me."

"Yes." She gave him the word, half in bitterness, half in the soft, yearning whisper of desire.

"Let's go with that, then, why don't we? With how much you want me. Let's not get it all bound up with…complicated emotions. We want each other. You called me. I came over. You've made it real damn clear that you're *not* in love with me. Still, there's no reason we both can't have…what we want."

But there *was* a reason. No matter what he said. If she took him to bed, it would change what they were to each other. Was she ready for that?

She had no idea. And that meant she should… argue some more, say something tough and un- flinching. She should push him away, ask him to please get dressed and go.

But, oh, what she *should* do and what she wanted so bad that wanting had a taste and a scent and a hard, hot feel…

Those were two different things.

And he was making it worse. Or better.

Or…whatever.

He was kissing her, light kisses, nipping, arousing kisses, down over her jawline, along the side of her neck. She shivered.

And she sighed.

He trailed a hand over the curve of her shoulder and inward, laying his palm, so lightly, against her breast. Even through her shirt and bra, her nipple seemed to rise to meet him.

She moaned, half in excitement and half in weak protest. "Not fair…"

"Too bad." He licked her neck, one long, slow

stroke. And he blew where he'd licked, so she shivered in delight.

She couldn't help herself. She really *had* to touch him. She grasped his bare shoulders, sighing at the pure pleasure of the contact, loving the sleek, hard feel of him as that taunting hand of his left her breast and began undoing the little white buttons down the front of her shirt.

It should have been so simple, shouldn't it?

To put a hand over his, to tell him, *Stop.*

One word, one quelling touch of her hand on his. Nothing to it.

But she didn't do it.

Instead she moaned again, as he peeled her shirt wide and guided it off her shoulders. She had to let go of him so he could get the sleeves down her arms.

He threw it over his shoulder. She didn't even care where it might land.

Next, he reached behind her. One-handed, he unhooked her bra. It went the way of her shirt.

And then he cupped a breast in his warm hand and lifted it. "Beautiful," he whispered. "More beautiful, even, than I remember...."

He lowered his head. She felt his warm breath on her skin. He took her breast, sucking, his tongue circling the nipple as he drew on it so sweetly and steadily....

She thought she would die of pure pleasure, right then. Right there...

He urged her down, onto the bed, and he came down with her. By then, it had all gotten…magical, somehow.

And dreamlike. And so very erotic.

She had no more thought of resisting him. Her own arguments of moments ago seemed foolish now. Pointless. Silly, even.

No woman in her right mind would resist pleasure like this.

He took away her jeans and her panties. In no time she was as naked as he was.

He touched her. Everywhere, those clever fingers stroking slowly, maddeningly, along the tops of her thighs, bringing goose bumps, eliciting soft moans and lingering sighs….

Slowly. Oh, yes. That was the word.

He took her so slowly. So patiently, that at each step she ended up begging, "Oh, please. Brand. More…"

His mouth found her breast again. He sucked on it, making her moan with the sheer delight of his tongue stroking her nipple. There was nothing like the warm wetness beyond his lips, the lovely, thrilling suction he created as he worked her nipple to an aching peak.

His fingers brushed along her thighs, over and over, until she was squirming, yearning for them to move higher….

She parted her legs for him, offered herself up to him.

And he claimed her mouth again, kissing her deeply, as his fingers moved closer to the place she couldn't wait for them to be.

He touched her, at last, those knowing fingers parting her, sliding in where she was wet and open and yearning. She cried out at the pleasure of that. And he stroked her, all along the hot, feminine heart of her. She lifted her body toward his pleasuring hand. She kissed him as deeply as he was kissing her.

Soul-kissing, they called it. Only with Brand had she understood the meaning of that word. They kissed forever as he played her below. She felt her body rising, reaching for the peak.

Shining seconds later she went over, pulsing, so hot. So right. She cried out into his mouth, and he drank the sound as part of that endless, deep, soul-burning kiss.

He had a condom. He rolled it down over himself. So thick, he was, so hard and hot....

She wanted to touch him, to stroke him, to bring him the same pleasure he'd given her. But when she closed her hand around his shaft, he caught her wrist.

"I can't," he muttered. "I have to..." Words seemed to fail him.

But she understood. His slow, deliciously maddening seduction of her body had worked its magic on him, too.

Now, all he wanted—needed—was to be inside her. And that was just fine with her.

That was right.

It was good.

Funny, but now, naked and flushed with excitement, as he kissed her, as he rose above her and settled between her open thighs…

As he pushed into her and her body—relaxed, satisfied, and yet, at the same time thoroughly aroused all over again—opened, welcoming, drawing him in….

At that moment everything was right between them, everything was good. All the old bitterness, the anger, the deep hurt, the sad, ugly animosity…

It was gone. All of it. Vanished. Pouf. It didn't exist.

He pushed in with a low groan and she took him, deep, all the way, lifting her legs and wrapping them tight around him. She met his thrusts and moved in answer, following his lead, crying out at the end as he pushed in hard, straining, and she felt him pulsing, felt her body tightening, finding release right along with him.

They went over the moon together. It was so good, so perfect.

No, she didn't love him. She never would. Never again. She could never trust her wounded heart to him.

Still, as the pleasure crested and she was lost in glorious sensation, she couldn't stop herself from calling out his name.

Chapter Twelve

Brand knew she would try to send him away as soon as her breathing evened out and the afterglow faded.

He knew she would start doubting again, start beating herself up for letting it happen, for taking the man she'd despised for a decade into her bed.

And that would be it. He'd be outta there.

He wasn't letting her send him packing if he could help it. No way. After all these years, he was finally back where he wanted to be. And he was totally shameless. Oh, yeah. Shameless. And proud of it. He'd use anything, *do* anything, to stay right there in Charlene's bed, wrapped up all warm and tight in her soft arms.

At least for the rest of the night.

He had zero illusions. His eyes were wide-open. He knew damn well that great sex didn't solve all the problems of the world. Far from it. She'd softened toward him; she was grateful that he was doing what he could to help her find Sissy.

But she hadn't forgiven him for turning his back on her a decade before. Maybe she never would.

Maybe he'd blown it for good back then and this—tonight, with Charlene naked in his arms. This was all he was getting, all she could give.

All the more reason, he figured, that they both deserved the rest of the night.

His mission was clear: to distract her, to give her no opportunity for remorse or regrets. It was a challenge he was only too happy to accept.

For starters, he licked the sweat from the side of her neck, caught her tender earlobe between his teeth and teased it. She moaned in protest and shoved halfheartedly at his shoulders—a woman satisfied and not ready to get worked up all over again.

He went on kissing her. He kissed her collarbones—a long, slow row of kisses, across the delicate shape of them. He kissed that tender hollow at the base of her throat.

She sighed when he kissed her there—and he knew he was making progress. Suddenly, instead of pushing at his chest, she was wrapping her arms around him, running those soft hands up and down his back.

He kissed his way up the side of her neck again,

traced the delicate hollows and curves of her ear, even dared to dip his tongue inside, to whisper her name, to tell her she was beautiful.

Which she was.

So slim and strong, with breasts a little fuller than he remembered them, with softly curving hips, dark gold curls between...

They had so much lost time to make up for. *He* had so much to make up for. And he would. Not matter what she said, he would earn her trust again.

He kissed his way down her body. When he eased under her thighs and settled her slim legs over his shoulders, she didn't protest.

All she said was, "Oh, Brand..." And a moment later, "Yes..."

Charlene woke at four when the baby monitor crackled to life with Mia's cries. She turned on the light automatically. About then, she remembered she wasn't alone in her bed. She glanced over her shoulder as Brand opened one eye.

He yawned. "Is it morning?"

"Technically, yes." She threw back the covers and tried not to think how he was watching her bouncing bare bottom as she zipped over to the closet and snared her robe from the inside of the door.

Mia cried louder.

Brand shoved the covers away and jumped up. "I'll help."

She made a point of not so much as glancing at his gorgeous naked body as she hurried past. "It's not necessary."

"Aw, c'mon." He bent and grabbed his boxers and was shoving his legs into them as she reached the door.

In Mia's room, Charlene switched on the small lamp to its lowest setting and bent over the crib. "Shh, honey. Here I am...."

The baby fisted her little hands and kicked her feet and let out another wail as Charlene unsnapped her sleeper to get at her diaper.

"What's up?" Brand leaned in the open doorway to the kitchen.

She slanted him a look as she lifted the baby from the crib. "She's wet. I'll change her. If that doesn't settle her down, I'll heat up a bottle."

He straightened and entered the cramped room. "Let me do it."

She hesitated, then shrugged. "Remember. You volunteered...." She passed him the fussing Mia. He carried her over to the changing table and set to work.

Charlene wrapped her arms around herself, nibbled her lower lip and stared at his broad back. There was just something about a hunky guy in red boxers bending over a cranky baby, gently unsnapping her sleeper along her plump little legs.

A woman could be a total sucker for a man who

jumped out of bed when the baby cried, a man who actually offered to change diapers—and then displayed excellent follow-through.

He hit the lever of the diaper pail with his toe. When the lid sprang up, he dropped the wet diaper in and let the lid drop. Then he cleaned Mia up with a baby wipe and put on a fresh diaper. Within two minutes, he was snapping her back into her sleeper again.

"You're pretty good at that," Charlene observed when he raised the still-fussing baby to his shoulder and patted her little back in an effort to soothe her.

"I've changed a diaper or two in the last year or so," he said. "I've got three nephews, after all." Each of his brothers had one baby boy. Though only Brett still lived in town, Buck and his wife and son came to visit now and then. Glory, who had Bowie's son, would accompany them.

"Well, I'm impressed."

"I'm a talented guy." As if in response to that remark, Mia let out an extraloud wail. Brand winced. "Watch the eardrums, there, gorgeous."

"She's hungry. I'll get a bottle ready...."

Brand wanted to feed her, so Charlene let him, silently reminding herself the whole time not to get too used to having him around, not to get all dewy-eyed over the sight of him, bare-chested and so handsome it hurt, sitting in the rocker with Mia in his arms.

Once she ate, she needed changing again. Brand

carried her right in and took care of it. Charlene returned to the bedroom, where he joined her a few minutes later.

He hesitated in the doorway. "I've changed two diapers and fed the baby. Don't you even think about sending me home now." He said it teasingly, but she could see the apprehension in his eyes.

By way of answer, she held back the covers for him.

He dropped the boxers on the floor again and slid in beside her.

She switched off the lamp and stretched out on her back and stared into the shadows near the ceiling, feeling him right there, beside her. So close she only had to reach out her hand.

She did just that, tentatively, touching the space between them first, then closer, until she brushed his hip. He took it from there, his warm fingers closing over hers.

"We can play it by ear," he said, his voice low and husky, coming out of the darkness at her side. "How 'bout that?"

"People will talk," she replied, still staring at the ceiling, smiling to herself as she realized that she really didn't care what people said about her and Brand. It was just something you had to consider in a small town like the Flat, something that you had to be aware of.

His fingers tightened over hers in a reassuring squeeze. "They'll talk no matter what we do."

She made a noise of agreement. And then she gave in to her own desire to be closer and curved her body into him.

His big arms encircled her.

It felt good, Brand's embrace. Really, really good.

Nothing lasted forever. Charlene had learned that hard lesson young. But for the time being, there was nowhere else on earth she'd rather be than right where she was, held close in Brand Bravo's cherishing arms.

The next day was Sunday. The diner was closed.

Charlene, Brand and Mia had breakfast at the B&B with Irma. Irma remained her new, lovely self. Brett's wife, Angie, called Brand on his cell while they lingered over second cups of coffee.

Angie invited Brand and Chastity for dinner.

Brand joked that he'd only come under one condition: Charlene, Mia and Aunt Irma had to be invited, too.

Angie said, "The more the merrier."

So they spent the evening at Brett and Angie's house down by the river. Brett barbecued chicken and Irma got to hold not only her grandniece, but Angie's baby, Jackson, too. He'd been born March 8, just a week before Mia.

Later, when Charlene was helping load the dishwasher, Angie remarked on what a "sweetheart" her aunt Irma was.

Charlene grunted and shook her head.

"What?" Angie bent to drop dessert forks into the flatware basket.

"Oh, nothing. My aunt is…a whole new woman lately, that's all. I'm kind of waiting to wake up one morning and find the old Aunt Irma has come back."

Angie flipped on the faucet and rinsed her hands. "You make it sound like that wouldn't be good."

Charlene almost changed the subject.

But she *liked* Angie. And Angie probably knew the basic story, anyway. Brett's wife had been a year ahead of Charlene in school and gone off to college before Charlene's folks died. Though Angie hadn't returned to live in town until last year, she had a huge extended family, including eight siblings. Most of them lived in the Flat. Charlene was betting Angie's mother or one of her sisters would have told her all about how Sissy had been sent away to live with an aunt in San Diego.

Charlene said, "Irma's the one who took me to court to get custody of Sissy."

"No."

"Yeah."

Angie reached for a towel and leaned closer to Charlene as she dried her hands. "I think I heard somewhere that the woman who took your sister was a raving bitch—no offense to your aunt or anything."

"Why would I be offended? It's the truth. Aunt

Irma *was* a raving bitch. Back then. And at least up until last Wednesday, when I called her on the phone and she said any number of cruel and unforgivable things to me. I still don't know exactly what's happened to suddenly make her the sweetest woman in California. Every time I ask what's going on with her, she puts me off. But she has…apologized, for how hard she was on Sissy, for how harsh she's been to me."

Angie hung the towel back on its hook. "Some people do just…wake up one day and see the light. Maybe that's all there is to it. Your aunt Irma has seen the error of her evil ways and decided it's time she made amends."

Charlene chuckled. "Is that your professional opinion?" Angie was a nurse. She worked with her husband, who ran the town clinic.

Brett's wife shook her dark head. "I'm afraid I'm just too cynical to buy that. My guess would be…" The words trailed off. She looked at Charlene sideways. "You know, on second thought, you don't need my opinion. That's all it would be, really. Just an opinion…."

Charlene sighed. "Look. Don't worry about freaking me out. I've already been thinking it has to be something awful that's snapped her out of a lifetime of pure, flat-out meanness, like maybe a terminal illness."

Angie gave a bleak shrug. "Or extreme emotional

trauma. That might do it. And then there's what you said at first…"

"Exactly. That she hasn't really changed at all, she's simply…up to something."

Angie shook her head. "I don't know. If she's faking it, she's really good. Because I buy it. She comes across as a truly nice person."

Charlene had to agree. "She does, doesn't she— and you know what? The more we talk about this, the more I like your first suggestion. Aunt Irma finally woke up and smelled the coffee. She caught a flight and came right to my house to try and make up for all those years of awfulness. For now, until I can get more information out of her, I'm going with that. And I'm also enjoying her." Charlene said that again. "Enjoying my aunt Irma. Now, there's something I would have sworn a week ago you'd never hear me say."

Tanner called the next evening, while Charlene and Brand were fixing dinner. Brand was peeling potatoes at her sink and Charlene was trying not to feel too ridiculously sappy and domestic, trying not to sigh over how well they got along together, trying to keep in mind that it wasn't forever, that nothing ever was etc., etc.—and besides, it hadn't even been forty-eight hours since she called him at nine-thirty at night and he obligingly came right over and carried her straight to bed.

She was watching him wield that potato peeler

and reminding herself for the hundredth time not to get too attached to this new thing with him, when the phone rang.

Tanner said, "I have some information to go on. I wanted to give you a brief report before I follow up."

Charlene's legs went to rubber. She lowered herself carefully into the nearest chair. Brand had stopped hacking at the potato in his hand and was looking at her, wearing a worried expression. She mouthed "Tanner" at him and then spoke into the phone. "Yes. Please. Tell me."

It *was* brief. He'd checked in all the Western states, using the various databases he had access to and found nothing on Sissy for the past year. "All that means," he explained, "is that she probably hasn't been arrested. She hasn't registered a car or gotten a parking ticket. She hasn't used any credit cards—not under her own name, anyway. She's pretty much dropped off the map."

"You're saying you've got nothing to go on, to try to find her."

"Not completely. I still have the phone numbers you gave me. I'm going to talk to that girl your sister knew in junior high, see if I can jog her memory a little." He said that the numbers from her phone bill were all cell numbers. It had taken a little extra digging, but he'd matched them to billing addresses. He'd cleared off his other commitments for a couple of days and was heading first to Southern

California and then to the Bay Area to knock on doors.

She asked, "You aren't going to just...call them?"

"Eventually. If I can't get through any other way. But first I like to get face-to-face, if I can. I learn a lot more that way. People have more defenses in place when it comes to the phone than they do when someone's at their door."

She confessed, "I tried all the numbers from that phone bill again. Night before last."

"Any luck?"

She went and got her notes and read them to him.

He thanked her and then gently advised, "Better if you don't call them again until I give you a go-ahead. If any of them do know something they're hiding, your calling will only remind them to be on their guard."

"Of course. I won't. I'm sorry, I—"

"Nothing to be sorry about. Brand says you don't want me interviewing your aunt, Irma Foxmire."

"That's right. It's...complicated."

"Hey. You're the boss on this. Just let me know if you change your mind."

"I will."

"I'll contact you as soon as I have something to report. And you can reach me anytime at the cell number on my business card." He said goodbye.

Brand had left the sink and come to sit in the chair next to her. He brushed a steadying hand against her shoulder. "What? Bad news?"

"Not really, no..." She repeated what Tanner had said, adding, "I don't know. I just keep getting the feeling I'm never going to see my sister again. And the idea terrifies me, Brand. It makes me feel powerless and sad and just so hopelessly frustrated. I want her to be safe. I want her to be...happy. But I'm just so afraid for her, you know? I'm just so worried her little girl will have to grow up without her, that something might have happened to her, that she's in some big trouble and there's no one there to help her, that it might even be too late, she could even be—"

"Hey," he said. "Hey..." He rose, took her hand, pulled her up into his arms.

She sniffed the tears away and buried her head against the hard warmth of his shoulder, and somewhere in the back of her mind, the old warning played as usual, in an endless loop.

Watch out, you can't trust him. You know you can't. He left you once, he'll do it again.

Charlene shut her eyes tight and ignored those warnings. She hugged Brand harder, grateful for his strength and support right then, when she really needed it.

He pressed his warm lips to the crown of her head. "Tanner will find her." He sounded so sure.

She clung to that, to his certainty. She reminded herself that it had only been nine days since the morning she found Mia on the sofa. Nine days wasn't that long. Sissy could turn up again any day now—and she'd sounded downright cheerful in that note she'd left, cheerful and thoughtless and determined to do things her way, as usual.

Not like someone in big trouble, not like a person who needed—or even wanted—help.

She lifted her head from the comfort of his shoulder and beamed him a wide, brave smile. "Okay. I think I've pulled myself together now. You can finish peeling the potatoes."

"Damn. Just when I was going to carry you off to bed and comfort you...intimately."

She considered. Because, actually, being comforted intimately by Brand didn't sound like a bad idea at all.

"Hmm," she said. "Mia's napping, the roast isn't done yet. And the potatoes really could wait a few more minutes. Let's see...could you make it fast?"

He pretended to take her question with great seriousness. "Comfort you. Intimately. And fast."

"Yes. That's it. That's what I want."

He laughed that deep laugh of his. And then he scooped her up against his chest and carried her to the bedroom.

For a while she forgot all about her lost sister and her currently motherless baby niece, about the strange transformation of her evil aunt Irma, even about the fact that she had to watch herself with *him,* she had to be careful, not let herself count on him too much.

Not get too attached.

For a while she forgot everything but the stunning, amazing feel of his hands on her body, and the wonder of having him moving inside her, and those kisses of his that went on forever.

For a while…

Chapter Thirteen

The week went by. Charlene's constant worry about her sister aside, it was a good week. She and Brand were together constantly. He spent every night at her house, and she welcomed him there.

What woman in her right mind wouldn't? He was only too happy to help with the cooking and cleanup; he fed and diapered the baby without even having to be asked; he made Charlene laugh; and he seemed to enjoy being around both Mia and Aunt Irma.

And then there was the fabulous lovemaking they shared. That just seemed to get better and better.

Charlene really was taking it a day at a time and doing a pretty good job of it, with Brand's help.

Irma remained at the B&B. She'd have breakfast in the dining room there and then come on over to the diner for lunch. She and Chastity were becoming friends. Sometimes when Charlene dropped by to see her, she'd find her out on the front porch enjoying the spring weather, laughing with Brand's mom.

Charlene's aunt showed no inclination to head back to San Diego. Thursday evening, when Chastity and Brand took the baby inside to give Charlene and Irma a few minutes alone, Charlene asked how Uncle Larry was getting along without her.

Irma only waved a hand and said, "Oh, you know Larry. He's always been perfectly capable of looking out for himself."

Charlene couldn't argue with that one. If there was one thing Larry Foxmire made sure of, it was that Larry got what Larry wanted. He'd always been cold and distant around Charlene. Sissy used to say that he was the meanest man on the planet—and self-righteous in his meanness, the perfect husband for awful Aunt Irma.

It was a mild evening, but it had grown a little chilly after darkness fell. Charlene drew her light sweater a little closer around her. "Aunt Irma?"

"Umm?"

"You really *have* changed, haven't you?"

"Oh." Irma stared off down the walk, toward Chastity's white picket fence and the steep sidewalk beyond it. "I hope so. I mean to. I mean to be…a whole new me."

"But, well, I'd really like to understand…."

"Hmm?"

"*Why?* What *made* you change?"

Irma looked at Charlene then. Through the nightshadows, Charlene watched her smile. "Does it really matter what caused the change, as long as it's happened?"

Charlene thought about that one. "Yeah. I guess it *does.* It always helps to understand why the people you care about do what they do."

"Ah." Irma spoke softly, with that new, amazing sweetness. "So you care about me now, do you?"

Charlene nodded, a little surprised that Irma would ask such a question. "Well, yeah. I do. I've always cared about you—even when I wanted to strangle you. You're my aunt. I may have wanted nothing to do with you, but I cared. I did. I always cared."

Irma reached across the distance between them and laid her hand briefly over Charlene's. "I think you're a little worried, that's all—worried that I'm up to something, that I'm plotting against you. I think maybe you're waiting for…the other shoe to drop, as they say. And I don't blame you in the least for that, for mistrusting me and my motives. Not after the abuse you and Sissy have suffered at my hands in the past…"

Charlene didn't know what to say. It was, after all, so exactly what she *had* been worrying about.

Irma chuckled. "Honey, I'm just not quite ready to talk about why yet. And I don't expect you to believe in me, I know I can't ask for that kind of blind trust. And I'm *not* asking for it. I'm only saying, the honest truth is, I really have changed. I have no idea what's happened with Sissy, but I know it's not good. I can see by the haunted look in your eye every time someone says her name, that wherever she is now, you're not comfortable with it. I'm, well, I'm worried sick for her—in spite of the terrible things I said to you when you called last week. Believe it or not, I was worried then, but I couldn't let myself show it. I wasn't ready to face how much I'm to blame for what's happened with your sister."

Charlene spoke in a stunned whisper. "And now…you *are* ready?"

"Oh, yes. I am. And there was a time when I would have gotten on my high horse and started trying to run everything. I would have been so sure that, wherever Sissy is, her little baby ought to be with me…."

Charlene sat very still. She had no idea what to say, how to respond, as her aunt sat there so calmly on Chastity's wicker settee and described in aching detail a good number of Charlene's deepest, darkest fears.

Irma was still talking. "Yes. It's true. There was a time when, given this exact situation, I would have tried to get custody of Mia. I would have told myself she was better off with me. I would have called Social Services, had her taken away from you if you refused to give her up to me. I would have done anything—*anything*—to prove that I was right. And of course, all the while, what I'd really have been doing was ripping our family apart. Same as I did ten years ago." Irma folded her hands in her lap and shook her head at them. "No. I think I want to go about this a different way this time. I think I want to be here, when Sissy finally does come home. I think I want to be…a support to you, Charlene. A help and not a hindrance. A true friend, not an enemy."

"Do you believe her?" Brand asked later that night in bed, after she'd told him everything her aunt had said.

"I *want* to…"

"I think I hear a great, big *but* in there somewhere."

She cuddled in closer and put her hand on his warm, hard chest. "Well, yeah. I'm reserving judgment. But I do like what I'm seeing. And if she keeps on like this, well, the day is bound to come when I actually do trust her."

"Scary huh? Learning to trust…" His voice was gentle. Full of tolerance and understanding. She knew he was talking about more than Aunt Irma. He added wryly, "Especially when you've been screwed over before…."

* * *

Tanner called at seven the next evening, Friday.

He'd been to visit all the addresses he'd found for the numbers Charlene gave him. Randee Quail had no more to tell him than he'd already told Charlene. The three cell numbers in San Diego were also former schoolmates of Sissy's. One of those, he caught up with at her parents' house; one was at UC Irvine and the third had an apartment in Hollywood.

All three claimed they hadn't seen or heard from Sissy in a year.

Charlene sighed. "But two of them told *me* they'd never heard of any Sissy."

"I mentioned that, once we got down to the truth, that they *did* know her. They all said Sissy had called them last year, after she left your place there in the mountains, and asked them to pretend not to know her if anybody called or came around with questions."

"But they ended up telling *you* that they knew her…."

He gave a dry chuckle. "That's part of what you're paying me for, to get people to talk. Unfortunately, what they said when they finally did talk hasn't been a whole lot of help in the main job of finding your sister—as of yet, anyway."

The guy with the no-longer-in-service number, Tanner said, was doing time at Folsom on a drug charge. He'd served eight months of a three-year sentence and claimed he hadn't heard from Sissy since before he went in.

"I pulled a few strings," Tanner continued, as Charlene tried not to get depressed over the thought that her sister was calling drug dealers. "The guy's had a visitor or two. Not Sissy, though. From what I could find out, he's had no contact with her since she called him last year."

All that left was Dwayne and Zooey in San Francisco. Tanner said he'd caught Dwayne alone and gotten a few interesting bits of information. "Dwayne Tourville was your sister's boyfriend in high school. His current girl, Zooey Nunley, never met her. Dwayne says he moved to the Bay Area two years ago, lives with Zooey in San Francisco now. He says that he's talked to your sister on the phone a few times since he left Southern California."

"Has he seen her?"

"Once. She dropped in on him back around the first of April. She had Mia with her and she was asking for money. He claims he gave her a hundred dollars and told her not to come around again. He seemed to think Zooey, who pays the rent, wouldn't be too thrilled about meeting an old girlfriend *and* her newborn baby."

"So my sister was in San Francisco, with Mia, a few weeks before she dropped her off with me...."

"Sorry, Charlene. I know it's not much."

She made herself ask the question that had crept

into her mind. "Do you think Dwayne might be Mia's dad?"

"I followed that line with him for a few minutes. He said no way and insisted again that, aside from her showing up at his door uninvited that one time a month ago, he hadn't set eyes on Sissy since he left San Diego."

"Did you believe him?"

"Can't answer that. The guy seemed a little hinky—but he's trying to keep Zooey from getting worried she's got competition from some old girlfriend. He lied when *you* called him, right?"

"That's right. He told Zooey he didn't know anybody named Sissy."

"So he freeloads off his girlfriend and he'll lie to protect his interests. Does that mean he lied when he said he wasn't Mia's dad? At this point, there's just no way to know."

"Any other news?" Charlene asked, trying to keep her hopes up.

"That's all for now, but I'll keep on it."

"Can you fax me a report to the diner, with all the names and addresses and everything you found out?"

"Sure thing."

Charlene thanked him and said goodbye.

Brand had muted the TV when the phone rang. Now he took one look at her face and turned it off. "Judging by the way your shoulders are drooping, I'm guessing there's a shortage of good news."

"We still have no clue where Sissy's gone—except that she was in San Francisco, with Mia, a month ago." She told him all that Tanner had told her.

The next day, when she got Tanner's report, Charlene ached to take off for the Bay Area—and then for San Diego. She wanted to pay a visit to Dwayne in San Francisco, see if she could learn more from him than Tanner had, even though she knew the odds of that were slim to none.

Plus there was Mia to consider. She didn't want to leave the baby, not even to go hunting her sister down—and dragging Mia all over the state just wasn't any kind of option.

So Charlene stayed put. She worked and she cared for her sister's baby. She hung out with her aunt, who remained at the Sierra Star.

And she and Brand grew closer. He stayed at her house most of the time. Her bathroom cabinet was half-full of his stuff, and he'd taken over a couple of drawers in her dresser and a third of her closet. Not that she minded his taking up her space.

She didn't. Not in the least. She thoroughly enjoyed having him around.

Another week went by.

Sometimes she'd watch Brand feeding Mia, or glance up to see him sitting across from her at her kitchen table of an evening, and she'd get to thinking how much the three of them were like a family.

Sometimes it was hard to remember that she had to watch herself with Brand, that she couldn't let herself count on him too much, that they were just playing it by ear after all.

It was only a one-day-at-a-time kind of thing.

Now and then she'd hold Mia and she'd catch herself on the verge of murmuring, "Your mommy loves you," which wouldn't have been a bad thing.

Not in the least. If only she hadn't been thinking at that moment of *herself* as Mia's mommy.

If only it didn't get easier as the time went by, to forget about Sissy, to start feeling as if things would be the way they were now indefinitely: Charlene and Brand and Mia, a makeshift family, a family that felt more real to Charlene as every day went by.

Another week passed. And another after that. And two more....

Aunt Irma made two trips to San Diego—brief trips, by plane. She was back both times within forty-eight hours. And she didn't explain why she was going—or why she seemed to be more or less living at the Sierra Star.

After the second trip, on Thursday night, the first of June, when Charlene sat with her aunt out on Chastity's porch, she asked, "Is there something wrong between you and Uncle Larry?"

"Oh, no." Irma sipped the cup of tea she'd brought outside with her. "Nothing's wrong in the least. In fact, for once, everything's right."

"But you've been staying here in town for over a month now. Is Uncle Larry...okay with that?"

"I wouldn't know." Irma set her cup on the wicker side table. "The truth is, your uncle Larry and I have decided to go our separate ways."

Charlene had suspected as much. Still, it shocked her to hear her aunt say it so calmly. So...pleasantly. "Aunt Irma. Are you sure you're...okay?"

Irma chuckled. "Do you know how many times you've asked me that since I came to stay in the Flat?"

"Several. And you always just say you're fine."

"Because I am. I have never been better and that is the absolute truth."

"Do you want to talk about it? Sometimes it helps, I think, to have someone to confide in."

"Not yet..."

Charlene almost laughed. "That's what *you* always say every time I ask you what is going on."

Irma's expression was downright beatific. "I *will* tell you, honey. I promise. All of it. Every last gory detail. Eventually. Please. Don't be angry. Be patient with me."

"Oh, Aunt Irma. I'm not angry. Honestly."

"I'm so glad to hear that."

Charlene nibbled on one of Chastity's amazing lemon muffins. She sipped her own tea and then confessed, "You know, at first, I wanted to know what was up with you because I didn't trust you.

Now, well, I just worry that you're keeping everything all bottled up inside."

"Don't be hurt," Irma said gently, "but I'm not keeping it bottled up. I've told Chastity everything."

"You have?"

"I just...feel better talking about it with someone of my own age, if that makes any sense, someone who's not in the family, you know? Someone who's just a friend. I'm trying so hard to be a better person. But I haven't completely banished my pride. I'm not ready yet for my own niece to know, specifically, what a terrible fool I've been."

Tanner would call every Friday. He never had much to report.

But finally, on June sixteenth, Brand's brother called to give her the news she'd been longing for. He'd found her sister.

Charlene bit back tears of hope and joy and demanded, "Tell me. Everything. Please."

Tanner explained that Sissy had called Dwayne a couple of days before—and reached Zooey. Sissy had evidently played it much too cagey with Zooey, refusing to give any information about herself, just rattling off a phone number and insisting that Zooey have Dwayne call her.

Zooey confronted Dwayne, and he told her everything. He also handed over the business card Tanner had given him. Zooey called Tanner, and Tanner explained how Charlene really needed to find her sister.

Zooey gave Tanner the phone number Sissy had left.

The number was a land line this time. Tanner had matched it with an Oakland address, an apartment rented by a Shawna Pratt. He'd been to the address that morning and observed Sissy emerging from the apartment and returning several hours later. Did Charlene want him to go ahead and make contact?

Charlene thanked him profusely and told him she'd prefer to do the rest herself.

"Good enough." He gave her Shawna Pratt's phone number and the address. "And if you don't mind a little advice from a pro…"

She already knew what he was going to say. "Don't worry. I remember. I'm not giving Sissy a chance to hang up on me and run off. I'm going there."

"Good."

Charlene tried to get her mind around the fact that this was really happening. At last. "Is she…you said you saw her. Did she look okay?"

"Yes. She looked healthy. Uninjured." He added, "She seemed…alert." And Charlene took his meaning: Sissy hadn't appeared to be strung-out on drugs. He said, "I took several pictures. I'll send them by mail, if that's okay, along with a detailed report."

"That will be perfect. Thank you. Thank you so much."

"Glad I could help. You should have it all Monday

or Tuesday. Give me a call if there's anything more you want me to do." She thanked him again for all his hard work and asked for the bill.

He said Brand was handling that.

"I'd like to see the bill anyway. Please."

He promised to send it.

Her hands were shaking as she hung up.

Brand, with the baby in his arms, came out of Mia's room where he'd been doing diaper duty. One look at Charlene's face and he knew something big had happened. "Okay. What's up?"

"Tanner found Sissy. We're going to Oakland. First thing in the morning."

Brand wanted Charlene to leave the baby with Irma and his mother.

"That way," he reasoned, "if Sissy demands we hand the baby over, we can tell her she'll have to come back to the Flat to get her. At least it'll give us some time to decide what to do to protect Mia."

Charlene knew he was right. She had no idea how her sister was going to behave. And Mia's welfare had to be the first consideration. But leaving her with Irma...

Was she ready to do that, to trust Irma that much?

Brand must have read her fears in her eyes. "If you're still nervous about your aunt, I'll talk to Ma privately, let her know that we're leaving Mia with her as much as with Irma."

Charlene had to admit it was the best solution. Brand called Chastity and explained the situation. Chastity promised the baby would be safe at the B&B until they returned.

Irma got tears in her eyes when they dropped Mia off at six the next morning. "I know what this means, your leaving this little darling with me." She cradled Mia close and gently rubbed her back. "You're counting on me, *trusting* me, at last. I won't let you down."

Charlene gave her and Mia a hug, wrapping her arms around both of them at once—and refusing to feel sneaky that she'd had Brand call Chastity.

But then, when she pulled away, Irma actually winked at her. "And I'm not the least offended that Chastity will be keeping an eye on me, either. I'm just pleased you've come this far toward realizing you can count on me."

Charlene couldn't help laughing. "Chastity wasn't supposed to tell you that."

Irma beamed. "Chastity tells me everything. After all, we're the best of friends."

Brand came down the stairs from Irma's room, where he'd dropped off a big load of baby stuff. "Ready?"

Irma, holding Mia, with Chastity at her side, stood on the porch to wave goodbye.

Irma called, "Tell your sister I love her." She was

tearing up again. "I know she won't believe it, but you tell her, anyway."

"I will, I promise," Charlene called as they went out the gate.

The drive took four hours. Charlene was too anxious to do a lot a talking, and Brand seemed to understand her mood. It was mostly a long, silent ride, with Charlene counting the miles, begrudging every minute it took to get to the apartment where Sissy was staying.

By the time they turned onto Sissy's street, every nerve in her body was on red alert. She sat forward in the seat, hands on the dashboard, as if by leaning in the right direction, they could get to Sissy quicker.

The street was clogged with cars, every space on the curb occupied, but Brand pulled into the driveway of Sissy's building and parked in front of one half of a two-sided garage. The garage door, painted a peeling powder blue, bore a sign that read Tenant Parking Only.

Charlene, who normally would have obeyed such a sign, couldn't have cared less at that moment that they were taking someone's space. She had the door flung wide and was jumping to the pavement before Brand pulled to a full stop.

He got out and met her as she came racing around the nose of Cherokee. It was one of those courtyard apartment buildings, single story, in a U-shape, powder-blue doors along either side, a cracked concrete walk running up the middle to meet another walk and more doors lined up in the base of the *U*.

The address Tanner had given Charlene was the second unit on the right. Three steps led up to the blue door, patches of brown grass on either side. A strange, scraggly looking cactus plant sat in a pot at the edge of the bottom step.

Since there was barely room for both of them at the door, Brand hung back at the base of the steps and Charlene marched up and rang the bell.

A thin, pale-skinned girl with long, straight black hair answered. "Yeah?"

Charlene forced a smile. "Shawna?"

"Yeah."

Oh, God. What to say? How to make certain this girl let her see Sissy. She should have—planned this better. She should have decided ahead of time on the perfect approach.

Shawna's dark eyes looked past Charlene and narrowed on Brand. "Okay. What?"

"I'm…I'm here to see Sissy Cooper. I'm her sister, Charlene."

Shawna swore. A very bad word to be coming out of such a young mouth. "I kicked that bitch out last night. She ripped me off for two hundred bucks and then she brought that loser Jet around here when I told her not to. Not putting up with that noise. Uh-uh."

"Please. We just need…a phone number or an address where we could reach her…"

Shawna laughed. "Are you kidding? I told you. I kicked her butt outta here. The girl is gone. Mooching off somebody else by now."

"But if you could just—"

"Sorry. Can't help you." She started to shut the door—but Charlene reached out and grabbed it. "Hey!" Shawna shoved at the door, but Charlene held on. "What is your problem?"

"Please. You said she stole your money. I'll be glad to pay you back, if only you can tell me some way to contact her."

Brand stepped up beside her then. It was a snug fit, the two of them on that small slab of concrete stoop, but, boy, was she was glad for his presence.

He had his wallet, open, in his hand. "Two hundred, you said?"

Shawna looked longingly at the inside of Brand's wallet, but then she shook her head. "You want to give me the money she stole, fine. But I still haven't got any information for you. She's gone. Like I said, all I want is for her never to come back."

Brand took out six fifties, folded them neatly in half and slipped them through the crack in the door. "If she calls or shows up, try to get a phone number from her."

Shawna still didn't reach for the money. In spite of her bad attitude, she seemed to have an honest streak. "That's three hundred. She only took two."

Brand didn't pull the money back. "If you can't

get a number from her, ask her to please call her sister."

Charlene was already fumbling in her purse for a scrap of paper and a pen. She scribbled down the numbers. "Here's my home phone and the number at my business. Please call if you learn anything, if she contacts you, if you hear from her. Please."

Shawna peered at Charlene as Brand continued to hold out the money. "You got her baby, huh?"

"Yes. I do…"

"That baby okay?"

"She's great. Healthy. Beautiful. Tell Sissy that, please. If you see her…"

Shawna took the money. "Okay. But I warn you. Don't go holdin' your breath or anything. Your sister's not likely to be coming around here again."

They were home by a little after four. They went to the B&B first to pick up Mia.

Irma came running out to greet them. One look in Charlene's face and she knew that the news wasn't good. She hugged Charlene and whispered kind meaningless reassurances, "It'll be all right, honey. You wait and see."

They put the baby's stuff in the car and hooked Mia into her seat and drove back to Charlene's.

Charlene felt numb. What next? she wondered constantly. Should she call Tanner back and ask him to start searching for Sissy all over again? Should she just let it be for now? Just take care of Mia and wait until Sissy finally decided it was time to come home?

The next day, Sunday, Charlene and Brand and the baby went over to the Sierra Star to have breakfast with Chastity and Irma. Charlene enjoyed the meal and the good company. The numbness of the day before was slowly fading.

They got back home at ten past eleven. Charlene put Mia in her playpen and sat at her desk to pay a few bills. Brand sat on the sofa with his laptop, catching up on something from work.

The phone rang at noon.

Charlene reached over automatically and grabbed the cordless extension off the corner of the desk. "Hello."

"It's me," said the sulky voice that haunted Charlene's dreams. "You taking good care of my baby?"

Sissy. Oh, God. At last.

Charlene clutched the phone in a death grip as her pulse went galloping and all the saliva dried up in her mouth. "Yeah." The word came out barely more a whisper. She swallowed, tried again—louder that time. "I am. Taking real good care of her. Oh, Sissy. I promise you. Mia's fine…"

Brand appeared at her side. He put a reassuring hand on her shoulder. She sent him a hopeful, desperate glance as she groped for a notepad and a pen.

"It's so good to hear from you. Where are you? When are you coming ho—?"

"Don't talk." Sissy cut her off. "Listen."

"But I just—"

"Charlene. Are you listening?"

"Yes. I am. Of course."

"Then this is the deal. I'm not ready to come back to Hicksville, USA, yet—let alone to handle trying to take care of Mia. I called because I talked to Dwayne and he said you had some detective after me. I want that to stop. I don't want anyone following me around, spying on me. You understand?"

"Yes. That's fine. But—"

"Just say it. Tell me you understand. No detectives."

"All right. No detectives. I understand."

"And I'm doing just great, I mean it. Don't worry about—"

"But, Sissy, I *am* worried. Are you okay? Are you—"

"I said, I'm fine. I know how to take care of myself. I'll be back in the Flat when I'm ready. You get it?"

"Yes, I—"

"Good."

"Sissy, I—" Charlene heard the click that meant her sister had hung up on her.

She sat there holding the phone to her ear, unwilling to break the connection, though she knew very well it was already broken.

After the dial tone started buzzing, Brand took the

phone, so very gently. He turned it off and pulled her up out of the chair and into his cherishing arms.

That night, he made slow, tender, extraspecial love to her. She cried at the end, holding him close, letting the deep, wrenching sobs have her. Brand didn't say anything. He cradled her in his strong arms and stroked her hair and waited until she'd cried herself out.

Then he pulled the covers over them, kissed her nose and whispered, "Go to sleep. You'll feel better in the morning."

Chapter Fourteen

A fat envelope arrived the next day from Tanner. Charlene looked at the pictures of Sissy and wanted to start sobbing all over again.

But at least she *did* look healthy. She'd let her hair grow out a little—and she'd stopped dying it purple. Still spiky and wild, it was her natural honey-brown now and reached her shoulders. Her face was bare of safety pins. And, as sulky and hostile as she'd sounded on the phone, she also seemed sober. Just to know she was alive and well, that she wasn't strung-out on drugs…

Well, that was something. In time, Charlene

knew, Sissy would come home. Now it was just a matter of waiting until she finally did.

Charlene could handle that, now she knew that her sister wasn't dead in an alley or anything. She would take care of Mia and she would wait. She could do that, she could *bear* that.

A detailed report was in the envelope, too. So was the bill. Tanner had charged twenty-five dollars an hour plus expenses. The work he'd put in had really added up. And she had a sneaking suspicion he hadn't charged his own brother full price.

She thought of that three hundred dollars Brand had handed over to Sissy's former roommate on Saturday. When she'd tried to pay him back, he'd refused to take her money. And he was always showing up at her door with bags full of groceries and baby supplies.

Really, it was too much, all he'd done for her. That evening she told him she wanted to at least help with the bill from Tanner.

"Not a chance," he told her. "We already talked about that when this started."

"Brand. It's a lot of money—and I'll bet he didn't even charge you full price."

"He knows where to come anytime he needs a good lawyer at way below the going rate." He toasted her with the beer he'd just pulled from the fridge. "My only regret is that what he found out didn't get us any closer to getting this whole thing settled."

"I know that Sissy's okay, at least. And that's important. That means more than I can ever tell you. And I'm serious. I insist. I want to—"

He set down his beer, caught her wrist and reeled her in. "Don't argue. I can afford it."

She made a face at him. "So can I."

He kissed the tip of her upturned nose. "I never said you couldn't. What I meant was, I *wanted* to handle this."

"I shouldn't let you…."

"It's done. It's fine. Let it be."

She caressed the side of his face, felt the warmth and the beard stubble and thought how dear he'd become to her. Again. After all these years. Who would have ever thought that could happen? "Thank you. I'll find some way to pay you back."

"I don't want paying back. What I have is yours."

It seemed a pretty…strong thing to say. Given the whole no-long-term-commitment thing they had going. But she let it pass. After all, now and then, she found herself feeling the same way. That they were…together in a much more permanent way than they'd ever talked about.

It wasn't so. And they should probably have a talk about that sometime soon, get the boundaries clear between them again.

But not now. Not when he was being so sweet and generous and all she wanted was to stand there in the kitchen with his arms around her for a lifetime or so—that or twine her fingers with his and lead him off to her bed.

She rested her head against his chest, felt the good, steady beat of his heart beneath her ear. "Oh, Brand. I just wish she'd come home."

He stroked her hair. "Yeah. I know…" Something in the way he said that, the way he let the words trail off alerted her. A strange little shiver of unease crept down her spine.

She tipped her head up so she could see his eyes. "Something wrong?"

He took her gently by the shoulders. "I don't know how to say this. I keep waiting for the right moment. It just never seems to come."

She scanned his face for clues. "What? Tell me."

"It's been two months since Sissy dropped Mia off with you."

She knew already that she didn't like where this was going. "Not quite two months. Not for a few days…"

He looked infinitely patient all of a sudden. "All right. It'll *be* two months this week."

She eased out of his light grip and moved back so she could lean against the sink counter.

"You're mad," he said.

"You make it sound longer than it is, that's all."

"Charlene…"

She folded her arms across her middle in a gesture even she recognized as defensive. "What?"

"You need to start considering how you're going to protect Mia."

She hugged herself tighter. "Protect her? I *am* protecting her."

"You *are* getting angry."

"I'm not. I'm really not." She said it too fast—and too loud. And she knew she did. "I…what, Brand? What exactly are you hinting at? I think you'd better just say it."

"All right. First of all, you need to change your locks—Sissy does have a key, right?"

Charlene gulped—and hedged, "Well. Yes, I suppose so."

That infinitely patient expression of his was looking a little strained. "You told me she had a key, remember? That first morning, when you found Mia on the sofa."

"Yes, okay. She has a key. What are you getting at?"

"She has a key, Charlene. You don't have an alarm system. She could let herself in here anytime and you couldn't stop her."

"I wouldn't *want* to stop her. She's my sister. My house is *her* house."

"I understand why you say that. And I think it's…admirable, that you've stuck by her all these years, no matter what she's done, that you've always kept your door open for her. But I think you need to admit to yourself that things are different now."

Her chest felt tight—as if a band of steel encased

it. She wanted to demand that he stop right there, leave it alone, drop the subject, let it go…

He did no such thing. "Charlene…" He took a step toward her.

She put out a hand. "Don't."

He backed off. But he didn't give up. "Face it. She could let herself in and walk out with Mia every bit as easily as she walked *in* with her two months ago. You need to change your locks and then you've got to start thinking about taking steps to either adopt Mia or to be declared her guardian. The way it stands now, Sissy could show up at any time and tell you she wants her baby back. You'd have to hand Mia over. And then your sister could simply…disappear again, same as she did last year, same as she did two months ago. Think about it. Come on. You and I both know you owe it to that baby not to let her do that."

Her heart galloped painfully and her mouth had gone cotton-ball dry. "I can't. I could never—"

"You have to think of Mia, Charlene. You have to face that there's no way your sister can give that baby a decent childhood, given the kind of life she's living, no way she can provide a good start for a baby, no way she—"

"No." Charlene just wanted him to stop. She wanted him to quit telling her this awful truth that she still wasn't ready to accept. She held her arms tight around herself and she shook her head, whispered again, "No. Uh-uh. No…"

He stepped closer.

She hung her head. "I can't, Brand. No way. Not yet. Maybe not ever…"

He dared to clasp her shoulders. "Charlene. Listen."

She made herself look at him. "Oh, don't you see? Don't you see what you're asking? I get to be…Aunt Irma now? It's ten years ago all over again, only this time instead of Aunt Irma taking my sister away from the only home she's ever known, it's me. Taking her baby from her. How could I do that?"

"It's not the same," he argued. "If you really think about it, if you put all that guilt you insist on carrying around with you aside, you'll know that it's not. You were a responsible person when you were eighteen. It would have been a hell of a job to take on, to bring up Sissy yourself. But if anyone was capable of that, you were. Sissy's not you. Sissy abandon—"

"Stop." She shook off his grip. "Just…don't say that word, okay? Any word but that. Please."

He put up both hands, palms out, and backed away a few steps. "Fine. All right. Sissy is a troubled young woman. She behaves irresponsibly, she—"

"Oh, come on. There are a lot of mothers who aren't the best they could be, a lot of young, confused mothers who just need a break from all the responsibilities that come with having a child. That doesn't mean someone should take their kids away from them."

"Charlene. It's a cycle, you have to know that. Bad mothers make troubled kids and troubled kids grow up to be bad parents. It goes around and around. At some point someone has to step forward and break the damn cycle."

"Like Aunt Irma did?"

He swore low. "How many times do I have to say it? This situation and what happened back then just aren't the same—or wait. Maybe they *are* the same. You've just got the parts mixed up."

"What do you mean, the parts?"

"Let Sissy take that baby off and try to raise her. *Then* it'll be ten years ago all over again. Poor Mia will get some serious bad parenting—just like Sissy did when Irma stole her away with the help of a misguided judge."

"No. Oh, no…" Charlene shook her head some more, as if continued denial could block out what he was telling her, could make it less true—and yes. She did know it was true. He had it right, as much as it hurt to hear it.

But how could she do that to Sissy? How could she even consider trying to take her sister's child?

"I know." She confessed it at last with a hard sigh. "I know you're right. I know that, unless Sissy makes some major changes in the way she lives her life, Mia won't have a chance if Sissy takes her away. But I can't…push my sister aside and take her place with Mia. I mean it, Brand. Don't ask me to. I can't."

"I'm *not* asking you." He said it so gently. And his eyes were so sad. "I'm saying what has to be said, that's all. It's not about me. Or you. Or even Sissy anymore. Now it's about Mia." He gestured toward the living room where Mia lay in her playpen, waving her arms and legs, making happy little cooing sounds. "It's about doing the best you can for that baby in there. It's about giving her a chance to grow up into a productive, responsible, reasonably happy adult."

"Oh, God. Why? Why does it all have to be so…impossible? Either way, whatever I choose, I lose. Screw my sister over—or mess up Mia's life. It's no kind of a choice."

"Just tell me you'll think about it."

"Oh, Brand…"

"Give it some serious thought. That's all I'm pushing for."

It was a perfectly reasonable request. She pressed her lips together and nodded.

"Well, okay," he said. "That's something. That's a start."

Chapter Fifteen

Brand arrived at Charlene's after work the next day to find a locksmith's van in the driveway.

A half an hour later the locksmith left and Charlene handed him a shiny new key. "Since you practically live here, anyway."

He took her in his arms—his favorite place for her to be—and kissed her long and slow and deep. The baby cooed in her playpen, and as far as he could see there was no big rush to get working on dinner.

They could kiss their way into the bedroom. He could take off the snug red shirt she was wearing, peel off those curve-hugging jeans. Already he was rock hard and aching.

Her kisses tended to do that to him.

He eased his fingers up under the hem of that tight shirt and caressed the baby-smooth skin of her lower back. She sighed.

But then she pulled back. "I've been thinking..."

"Kiss now, think later." He lowered his mouth to capture her lips again, but she evaded it.

"You know I like nothing better than kissing you."

"Prove it."

"But..."

He groaned and gave it up. "All right. You've been thinking. About what?"

She skimmed a palm down the side of his arm and captured his hand. "Come on. Want a beer or something?"

"Hell. Why not? If I can't take all your clothes off and do bad things to your body..."

"You can. Later."

"Promise?"

"Oh, yeah." She led him to the antique couch under the big window and pushed him down. In a moment she was back with his beer.

He took it. "Okay. What's going on?"

She dropped down beside him. "I was awake half the night."

He made a show of rolling his eyes. "Tell me about it."

"I didn't mean to keep *you* awake."

"I kept waiting for you to speak up and say what you were thinking about."

She gave a small, nervous laugh. "And I kept trying not to toss and turn so I wouldn't wake you."

He bent to set his beer on the coffee table and dropped his new house key beside it. "And you were awake because…?"

She shifted on the sofa cushions. "I was thinking. About what you said last night."

He'd figured as much. And he was glad. She needed to start actively dealing with the giant-size problem that confronted her. He hadn't really expected her to get right on it like this, he'd figured he'd have to give her a nudge now and then for a week or two before she'd go anywhere with what he'd suggested.

Apparently, he'd underestimated her. Which was good. Great, even. They could finally get moving on making sure Mia was safe and provided for.

She smoothed both hands along her thighs, as if easing wrinkles from those tight jeans. "I made some decisions."

"Good."

"I decided you were right about the locks."

"And you took care of them," he added, with real approval.

"No way could I allow Sissy to sneak in here and run off with Mia. But as for the rest of it, the whole idea of trying to adopt Mia, or set up some kind of guardianship, well, no. I can't do that. Not until Sissy comes back, anyway. Not until she and I have a chance to talk about it, not until we get a few things settled between us."

He couldn't believe what he'd just heard. "Listen to yourself."

She stiffened. "I'm not necessarily expecting you to agree with me."

"Good. Because I don't. And what's this about getting a few things 'settled' with Sissy? As if she's the kind of person you sit down and have a long heart-to-heart with. I'm sorry, Charlene, but you're lying to yourself. And I seem to remember more than once you've told me you're afraid Sissy will *never* come back."

"Well, that's a fear. Yes. And a real one. And if she doesn't return in the next few years—"

"Few *years?* You can't—"

"Do you mind if I finish what I was trying to say?" She waited, blue eyes daring him to cut her off again.

"Go for it," he muttered darkly.

She brought up her hands and rubbed at her temples, as if dealing with him was giving her a headache. "Okay," she said finally. "I understand that eventually I might have to make some other plans. I might even have to take another chance with Social Services, put Mia's welfare on the line and try to get formal custody of her."

"Is that it?" He'd said he wouldn't interrupt, but this was a point that really needed making. "Is that the problem? You're afraid if you try for custody, someone will take Mia away from you, that it'll be like before, when your parents died? Because I meant it when I told you I can keep that from happening. You can count on me this time, Charlene. I promise you, no one will take that baby away from you."

"There's no absolute guarantee you'll be able to keep that promise."

"I'll be able to keep it. I swear to you."

"And where would that leave Sissy?"

"What do you mean, where would it leave Sissy?"

"I mean, we'd have to use that word I hate, wouldn't we? We'd have say she *abandoned* Mia. That's against the law, isn't it? Abandoning a baby?"

"Let's not—"

"Stop. Don't give me any lawyer double-talk. We'd have to say she abandoned Mia. And that would mean she'd not only lose her baby without having any say in the matter, she'd also be in trouble with the law."

"No. You're wrong."

"Oh, come on. She would. We both know that she would."

"That's just not so. Mia wasn't harmed or endangered by Sissy's actions. She left the baby with you, in your house. Safe. Your sister won't be charged with anything."

"Well, beyond being an unfit parent, you mean."

She is *an unfit parent,* he longed to say. But he took a more diplomatic tack, repeating what he'd told her a number of times, in hopes that maybe this would be the time she'd finally hear him. "All we're going to do is make sure that Mia gets the best care possible."

There was a silence. She regarded him—a long, slow look. "I *have* been wondering, at least a little…"

"What? Tell me. Ask."

"A minute ago you said I could count on you *this time.*"

"That's right. And you can."

"Are you sure all this—how good you've been to us, to Mia and me, how helpful. How kind. Are you sure it's not all just your way of making up for what happened when we were kids?"

He had to hesitate before tackling that one. He *knew* it had to be some kind of trap. A woman-type trap. Whatever he answered, he'd get it wrong. Because damn it, he *was* trying to make up for what had happened in the past. And he wasn't ashamed of that.

Was there some reason he *should* be ashamed?

She cleared her throat—just to remind him she was still waiting for a reply.

So he gave in and went with the truth—carefully. "Yeah. Making up for ten years ago is a factor."

She frowned, as if he'd just said some word she didn't understand. "A factor?"

"I've told you. I regret not sticking by you then— looking back, I'd say walking away from you is the worst thing I ever did in my life. I've never gotten past it, never forgiven *myself* for turning my back on you. But I just...wasn't *ready* then, to be what you needed me to be. I know—as much as I regret the choice I made then—that if I'd made the other choice, if we'd gotten married, I'd have screwed it up royally."

She just looked at him.

With a hard sigh, he took it farther. "You know how it was for me. I had to kind of...grow up on my own. My dad, who rarely came around for more than a few weeks a year, disappeared completely when I was barely two years old. I've got no memory of the man. Zip. I know him only from the ugly stories people tell about him, from the newspaper articles that called him a kidnapper, a psychopath and a murderer.

"And Ma's a great woman, she did the best she could for us. But she was damned preoccupied, trying to raise four boys and run a business on her own. She was in some faraway place in her mind most of the time when I was a kid, dreaming of the day my crazy dad would come back to her, even though she never had a real marriage with him. I had no example of how that might work—a man, a woman, partnering up to make a better life for themselves and their children. I just had no clue how to be a husband. And I certainly had no idea how to be a substitute father to a nine-year-old kid."

"Oh, Brand…"

What do you know? If her dewy-eyed expression was any indication, communicationwise, he'd just hit a home run. "Uh. Yeah?"

She smoothed the nonexistent wrinkles in her jeans again. "We've talked about my forgiving you…"

Hope rose in him, fizzy and light. Something told him this was the moment he'd been waiting for. He gulped. "Yeah?"

And she said it. "I do forgive you, Brand. I couldn't do otherwise. You've been so good these past weeks. To me. And to Mia. To Aunt Irma. You've made what started out as a terrible thing into something…so precious and special."

That was good, right?

Really good.

So why was the hope within him kind of fizzling? She forgave him. She'd said it right out loud.

But it was like a testimonial. Too much like the kind of thing a woman tells a guy just before she says it's over between them. He was way far from ready for it to be over—and wait a minute.

What was he worried about?

The key she'd just given him was right there on

the table in front of him, next to his beer. A woman didn't hand a guy a key one minute and tell him goodbye the next.

"So…" He sought the right question. "Where are we goin' here?"

"I'm just trying to tell you, if you felt you had to make up, somehow, for the past—you've done it. I'm through dwelling on that. What happened then, happened. Like you said last night, we've got to focus on what we're going to do now."

"And that is…?"

"Nothing." She looked so pleased with herself. "I changed the locks. Sissy won't be sneaking in here. Now all we have to do is wait. Eventually she'll show up. The rest of it we can deal with when she gets here."

Brand let it go at that.

What the hell else could he do?

He could make suggestions, try to nudge her toward the right choices. But he couldn't tie her down and force her to do what he thought was best.

It wasn't like they were married or anything. It wasn't like he had any real say in the choices she made in her life.

And why did that suddenly bug him so much?

She'd just told him he'd earned what he'd been wanting for years: her forgiveness. He slept in her bed every night, made love to her every chance they got. He was…happy, damn it.

Happy in a way he hadn't been since the first couple of years they were together back in high school.

What more was he looking for?

What else *was* there, anyway?

They made dinner. Ate. She cleaned up the kitchen while he fed and changed the baby. Once Mia was in her crib, they watched a couple of news shows and then headed for bed themselves.

There was only one sink in her bathroom. He brushed his teeth first. Within a couple of minutes he was undressed and sliding between her cool, white sheets.

He lay there, hands laced behind his head, waiting for her to finish doing all those things that women think they have to do at bedtime—mysterious and sweet-smelling procedures involving an impressive array of creams and lotions. On the dresser, the baby monitor made a nearly unnoticeable static sound, a constant, low sighing, like the sea in a shell. It was pleasant, that sound.

Soothing.

The bedroom door was open and so was the door to the bathroom. He could hear water running in there. The water stopped. He closed his eyes, imagined what she might be doing now: rubbing lotion on one of those pretty legs—or maybe brushing that gold hair, her breasts lifting under her robe as she raised her arms to stroke the long, silky strands.

It turned him on, just thinking about her in the other room, getting ready to join him in bed. *She* turned him on. Always had. Even all those years when she hated him, just the thought of her could get him aching, longing for the touch of her, for the sweet, fresh scent of her…for everything he was never going to have again.

Or so he'd always thought. Until Sissy left her baby on the couch and vanished. And all at once, out of nowhere, when he'd given up all hope it could ever happen, he was getting his second chance with Charlene.

He heard the whisper of bare feet and opened one eye to see her hovering in the doorway, her face scrubbed clean of makeup, all dewy and pink, her hair brushed smooth, shining on her shoulders.

"Come to bed." His voice was husky, betraying his eagerness to have her in his arms.

Still, she held back. "You look so peaceful, lying there…"

He cast a significant glance along the length of his body—down to the bulge in the blankets over his hips. "Not all *that* peaceful—get over here."

With a soft laugh, she came and stood by the side of the bed. He ached all the harder as she untied the sash of her robe, gathered it into a ball and stuck it in a pocket. The robe, hanging loose now, revealed a tempting section of her—the middle section— from her smooth upper chest, down between the twin swells of her breasts, to the hollow beneath her ribs and the sexy indentation of navel. Below that, there was the shining tangle of dark-gold curls, the matching sweeps of inner thigh....

He scooted higher against the headboard to get a look at the rest—at the tempting inside curves of her knees and calves. The robe ended just above her ankles. He admired her well-shaped, slender feet. Her toenails were painted hot pink.

"Take the robe off," he said. "Real slow."

Charlene was an independent woman. But, damn, she could follow instructions when she wanted to. She teased him a little first, laying her hand at the base of her throat, rubbing the silky skin above her breasts, stroking with her fingers, so lightly.

Brand dragged in one slow, deep breath. The scent of her came to him. So sweet. Clean. As arousing as the sight of her.

She traced a slow path down one side of the robe, skimming her own flesh with the movement, but somehow managing not to ease the robe open any wider...

"You're killing me," he told her.

"In a good way?"

"Oh, yeah..."

At last she took a little pity on him. She grasped one side of the robe and guided it over her shoulder. It slipped down her arm. One full, ripe breast, the nipple temptingly puckered, came into view.

Brand considered the possibility that he might just explode. Right then and there, without even touching her. "Let it slip off...only on that one side."

She obeyed, easing her arm free. The robe dropped away down her back, anchored now on her left shoulder. She was so beautiful. So shapely. He admired the sleek swell of her hip, that singing inward curve of her waist.

The covers weighed on him. He pushed them away, swung his legs over the edge of the mattress and sat on the side of the bed.

Her full, wide mouth was softly parted. She licked her upper lip, shy pink tongue darting out, swiftly vanishing again behind those lips he would soon be kissing.

"Come closer," he whispered.

She took a step.

"One more..."

She complied.

That brought her near enough that he could reach out and touch her. At last.

He did, with an index finger, tracing the line of that robe on the left side, following it down...

Her belly tightened as he skimmed it. He smiled up into her eyes and took his finger lower.

She gasped.

Good. He wanted her gasping. He wanted her pliant and willing and wild.

He touched the nest of shining curls where her

thighs met. She sighed. He eased his finger downward, within the curls, finding her cleft.

She was wet. Real wet. Ready-wet. They were so attuned to each other now, after all the nights of pleasure they'd shared. She didn't need a lot of foreplay.

Though they both *enjoyed* a lot of foreplay. Often.

Right now what *he* needed was for her to come even closer.

He grasped her waist with his other hand and pulled her to him. The robe slipped from her shoulder and plopped to the rug.

Fine with him.

"Kiss me, Charlene…"

She put her hands on his shoulders and lowered that wide mouth.

Oh, yeah. Kissing Charlene. Nothing like it. The taste of her, all sweet and wet. And her silky hair so warm to touch, flowing forward, brushing his chest. He speared his fingers up into the thick waves, making a fist, getting a big handful of it, so fine to touch…

All of her.

Fine to touch.

He pulled her closer. She came to him, keeping her mouth locked with his, hitching one slim leg up, shifting, lifting the other.

She straddled his lap, her weight to either side of him, up on her knees on the edge of the mattress.

Since she'd gone on the pill a month ago, they didn't have to worry anymore about the hassles of on-the-spot contraception. He was real glad about that at the moment. He was enjoying the erotic agony of straining upward toward her, seeking the soft, hungry heat of her body, knowing he wouldn't have to stop to deal with a condom.

Never once breaking their wet, hot kiss, she reached down between them and wrapped her hand around him.

He couldn't hold back his deep, pleasured groan. "Charlene…"

She stroked him. She knew just the way to drive him crazy, tightening her grip at the base, easing it in the middle, and then tightening again as she reached the top, rubbing the crown with her thumb, spreading the thick moisture that wept from the tip, until he was dropping his head back, lifting his hips to her, begging her with his body to give him what he sought.

At last, she did, positioning him, then lowering herself by slow degrees. He thought he would die.

And he didn't care—he was happy to go.

He groaned into her mouth as she settled onto him fully, so wet and hot and tight, all around him. And then he caught her hips and lifted her. *She* groaned then, as he pulled her back down onto him—all the way down.

From there on he was lost. Cast adrift in a lapping

wet sea of overwhelming sensation. He kissed her mouth and her breasts, sucking the nipples in, circling his tongue on them, as she held his head to her chest, riding him, whispering frantically, "Oh, yes. Brand. Yes…"

She lifted those fine hips of hers and lowered them, the sweet, wet friction so maddening, so perfect, so exactly what he craved.

He felt his body rising, felt the slow heat thickening, brimming—and finally spilling over.

She took him, her body milking him, holding him tight, crying out her completion as she came, too.

He collapsed back across the bed, pulling her with him. She landed limp on top of him, curled against his chest, her fragrant hair spread over his shoulders, sliding like warm satin against his throat.

What was it that happened then? Something… broke wide open inside him.

It was like a light blinking on in a pitch-black room, blinding in its sudden brightness.

The light of knowing. Of understanding.

What he wanted.

What he needed.

What, at last, against all odds, he finally realized he *could* do. And do well.

Amazing. But he could. He knew it now. With this woman. He could do it. He could do anything.

He smoothed her hair back over her shoulders. "Charlene?"

"Umm?"

"Charlene."

She dragged her head up and looked at him through lazy-lidded eyes. "What?"

He took her beautiful face in both his hands, pressed a quick kiss on her full lips. "Charlene..." He reveled in the simple sound of her name on his lips, in the weight of her body on top of him, in the musky, sexy scent of her after lovemaking.

She looked a little worried now. "Brand. What? What's the matter?"

"Not a thing."

"Then what's going on?"

And he said it. The impossible. The one thing he'd always known he could never say. He said it.

"Marry me, Charlene."

"Oh, Brand." She looked as if she might burst into tears. He grinned up at her, waiting for the answer he knew was coming. And then she said, "No."

Chapter Sixteen

Brand repeated blankly, "No?"

Rather than answer, she slipped away from him. He lay there, on his back on the bed, feeling like an idiot, like a hundred kinds of total fool.

She scooted to the edge of the bed, scooped up her robe and put it on again. He sat up as she was wrapping the sash around herself, pulling it snug, tying it tight.

"I'm sorry," she told him, and he could see in those blue eyes that she really was.

Sorry.

And certain.

He hadn't even tried to argue yet, but he knew

already that there was no way he would get her to change her mind. And he felt pretty damn stupid lying there buck-naked in the wake of such a flat-out refusal.

Never ask a question to which you don't know the answer. Primary lawyer's rule.

He'd gone ahead and done it, anyway. What a dumb-ass, blind fool.

He sat up—and she jumped back, as if afraid he would touch her, hold her, do something ter-rible…like pressure her to change her mind.

Okay, he needed a moment. He really did.

He went to the bureau and got a fresh pair of boxers. He turned his back to her, shook them out and shoved his legs into them. Once he had them on, he rested an arm on the bureau top and stared at the wall for a solid count of ten.

When he finally faced her again, she hadn't moved. She stood a few feet from the bed, wrapped in her robe, hands at her sides. "Brand. I'm sor—"

He put up a hand. "I heard you the first time."

"I'm…" She caught herself before she said it again. "I just can't, okay?"

He knew he shouldn't ask—but he did want to know. He wanted to understand. "You can't because…?"

"I'm just…used to it, you know?"

"It." He repeated the pronoun and waited for her to tell him what it stood for.

"I'm used to…taking care of myself, to *counting* on myself. Marriage, to me, means forever. And I'm not…I mean, I can't…" The awkward explanation died away unfinished.

And all at once, he understood. He *got* it. "You don't trust me. You *still* don't trust me."

"No. I didn't say—"

"You didn't have to say it. You don't trust me, Charlene. You've forgiven me, maybe. You don't hate me anymore. You even like me. You *want* me. But you're afraid to take any big chances with me. Day to day with me is okay. You just don't want to let yourself count on me. You're afraid I'll let you down again."

"I'm not afraid," she insisted. But all at once she was looking everywhere but at him: at the floor; at the rumpled bed; at the wall behind him.

If he'd had any doubt as to his assessment of the situation, they vanished. He knew from her refusal to meet his eyes that he'd hit that nail squarely on the head.

"You *are* afraid," he said.

Still, she tried to deny it. "No. Really. It's not that." She looked at him then. But not in his eyes— more like in the general vicinity of his chin. "It's not that."

"Yeah," he said. "It *is* that." And wondered what, exactly, he was going to do about it—if there was anything he *could* do about it. Should he swear he would stick by her, get down on one knee and beg her to give him a chance? Declare undying love and unending devotion?

He'd done a lot of that—of swearing he loved her, *would* love her forever—back when they were kids. And look how he'd ended up proving it.

By leaving her flat.

"I just can't," she said again, softly. Hopelessly.

From the monitor there came a tiny cry. And then a louder one.

Charlene said, "I should—"

"I'll get her," he said. "Go on back to bed."

Charlene did get in bed. And then she waited, sitting up against the headboard with the light on, for him to return.

When he came back in, she made a point to meet his eyes. "Okay," she admitted. "You're right. I'm afraid. I'm scared to death that if let myself start thinking this is permanent…"

"Then what?"

"You'll dump me again."

He stood in the doorway, so gorgeous and manly, wearing only his boxers, and he shook his head at her. "But I won't dump you."

"I hear you. I even…believe you." She touched her forehead. "In here—but in here?" She brought her hand over her heart. "I just…well, I'm too scared. I truly am. I…I appreciate everything you've done.

You've been wonderful, truly. And, Brand, I'm so grateful."

"Charlene. Take my word for it. I don't want to hear how damn *grateful* you are."

"I...okay."

"What else, then?" he bleakly demanded.

Oh, how to tell him? How to get him to see... "I'm crazy for you, Brand. Just wild over you. I think...I always have been. Even when I hated you, I couldn't get you off my mind. It's what you said to me that night we made love again for the first time. About the opposite of love being indifference, about how I've never been indifferent to you. I haven't been indifferent, not ever. I hated you to keep myself from admitting I was still crazy over you. I have been, am and probably always will be nuts over you."

He folded his big arms over that amazing, smooth, muscular chest of his. "But you're not going to marry me." It wasn't a question.

"That's right. I'm not."

"Because you still don't trust me—not really. Not in your heart, where it counts."

Her throat had a lump the size of a boulder in it. She gulped that boulder down. And she confessed, "You're right. I don't trust you not to...turn your back on me again. I don't trust you to stick by me forever. I've...lost too many people I love. My parents, my sister. You."

"But you *haven't* lost me," he told her so softly. "I'm right here."

She shook her head. "I know I should be braver. Stronger. I should be willing to take another chance. But I think it would kill me, Brand, if you stomped on my heart again."

He didn't answer for a moment. He stood there by the door, unmoving, his handsome face closed to her. Finally he said kind of wryly, "I'm guessing my swearing that you *can* count on me, that I *will* stick by you, just isn't going to cut it."

She *almost* said she was sorry—again—but shut her mouth over the words in the nick of time. "No. It's not going to cut it."

"I figured as much."

There was a silence. One that seemed endless and echoing. They stared at each other. The short distance between them was a chasm, miles and miles wide.

Then he spoke again. "The truth is, Charlene, you *can* count on me. You've *been* counting on me in the past two months. And whether you can get beyond all those crippling fears of yours or not and say yes to me, you're still going to be able to count on me. I'm going to see to that. I'm not the mixed-up, fatherless boy I was ten years ago. I know who I am now. And I know what I want. And that's to live my life with you."

She pressed her lips together to make them stop quivering. "But?"

A sad smile flitted across his wonderful mouth—and was quickly gone. "I'm not quite to the *buts* yet."

"I see."

"I don't think you do."

"I…"

"Charlene. I still want to help you any way I can. Legally. Or if you need money. Anything. Whatever you need, just say so. Just let me know. I mean that. Sincerely."

Her throat was clutching again. She gulped, asked him for the second time, "But?"

"Fine. Bottom line? I know we said we'd take it day by day. And I was okay with that. For a few weeks. A month. But I'm not willing to hang around here, playing house with you, counting on the fact that maybe someday you'll be ready to try again for real with me. I'm just…not up for that. I'm too proud. And even more than my pride, I know it would hurt too damn much. I guess it's my turn to say I'm sorry now. And I am. Damn sorry. I'm also heading on back to my own big, expensive, empty house."

Her heart thudded heavily under her breastbone. And she ached—to jump up, run to him, throw her arms around him. To beg him to stay, to promise him anything.

Anything. Even the lifetime he said he wanted, the forever that they'd lost before, the happily-ever-after that scared her to death.

If he'd only stay with her. If he just wouldn't go.

She didn't jump up, though. She sat right where she was, alone in her bed, hands folded tight on top of the covers, waiting…

As he went to the bureau and got out a T-shirt, pulled it on over his head. He got jeans, socks, boots from the closet…

In no time at all, he was dressed.

He said, "I'll come by tomorrow, when you're at the diner. I'll get all my things. I'll leave the key on the kitchen table."

She made herself nod. "Yes. Of course. That will be fine."

"And I mean it, Charlene. I'm not angry at you. Believe that, okay? Even if you can't believe in the two of us, in what we could have together, in what we could *be*."

"I understand. I know you're not angry." She coughed to clear the tears that were clogging her throat and she told him, "I do. I believe that. I honestly do."

"If you need me for anything, you call me. You hear me?"

She nodded again. "I will."

"Swear it."

"I swear it. I will."

He went out, closing the door softly behind him.

Chapter Seventeen

A week went by.

And another after that.

All of a sudden it was July. The nights were still chilly and the river was too cold to swim in.

Still, the days were long and lazy and warm. The kids were out of school, and constantly running in and out of the diner, getting cold drinks to go.

Independence Day came and went. Charlene watched the town parade go by beyond the diner windows. She skipped the Fourth of July dance that night, though even from up at her house a half mile away, she could hear the music playing down in the town hall.

She tried not to wonder if Brand was there, tried not to picture him dancing, holding some other woman in his arms, someone sweet and pretty, someone ready to say yes where Charlene had said no. She tried to tell herself it would be for the best, if he found someone else. If she saw them together, if all the folks in town started talking about Brand and his new girl.

If he had someone else, maybe she'd start getting used to the whole idea that she'd really lost him, that he wasn't coming back to her. Because he wanted more from her than she could give him now. He wanted her trust and a promise of forever.

And she just wasn't up to that—to trusting in forever. She didn't believe in forever anymore.

Three times she'd seen him on the street since he left her. Each time he had nodded and smiled. She nodded and smiled in return—and they both kept walking.

Yeah. She wished he'd get a girlfriend, at the same time as she knew that, if he did, she couldn't bear it.

In the meantime she ran her business. She took care of Mia, who continued to be the sweetest, most contented baby in the world. She waited for Sissy to come to her senses and come home.

The day after the Fourth was a Wednesday. Irma called Charlene at the diner.

"I have good news and I'm feeling festive. So how about a nice, big steak at the Nugget? Chastity says she can look after Mia."

"You know what? I've got a couple of steaks in the fridge. Nice ones. We don't need to go out."

"Well, I know that, but—"

"I could really use a good bottle of wine to serve with the steaks, though…"

"Honey. Are you certain? Because I'd love to take you out."

"Positive. What do you say? Six-thirty?"

"I'll be there. With wine."

Irma brought a very good Cabernet and opened it when she arrived. She poured two glasses. Then she detoured back to the living room to take Mia out of the playpen for a kiss and a cuddle.

From the kitchen Charlene heard her happily chirping, "All right, my darling. You just lie back down. Great-aunt Irma has important news for your Aunt Charlene."

Humming to herself, Irma returned to the kitchen and braced her hands on her slim hips. "Stop fiddling with the salad," she instructed. "Get over here and join me in a toast."

So Charlene dried her hands and joined Irma at the table. They both raised their glasses. "To…?"

Irma beamed. "To my bright and shining future here in the Flat, where I have at last discovered what really matters in life."

"Here's to that." Charlene clinked her glass with Irma's and then sipped. "Yum. Excellent."

Irma took a sip, too. "Oh, yes. Very fine." Then

she giggled like a girl. "I've been just dying to tell you. I bought that tumbledown old house three doors up from the Sierra Star."

"The old Lockhart place? No one's lived there for six years…" Charlene didn't know whether to congratulate her aunt—or offer condolences.

Irma laughed again. "I know, the house is a complete disaster. Lucky, lucky me—since I'm getting a nice, fat settlement from Larry, I mean. We are talking millions here."

"You're serious. He's worth that much?"

"He's not worth squat. But he's rich. I plan a total renovation. Inside and out. Should be quite an adventure."

"Oh, no kidding."

"And in the meantime, I'll stay at the B&B with Chastity." She set her wineglass on the table and clapped her hands. "I am so happy, honey. I just can't tell you. I just can't explain."

Charlene nodded. "And I'm happy for you." She set down her own glass.

"Oh, thank you. I'm happy for me, too."

Charlene held out her arms. Her aunt moved into them. They shared a nice, long hug.

When Charlene turned for the sink again, Irma said softly, "And you know that I want to be happy for *you*."

Charlene began cutting a tomato into wedges. "I'm fine. Honestly…"

Irma picked up her wine again. "You are such a

bad liar. You know you miss that man terribly. And I know without having to ask him, that he misses you. Whatever went wrong between you—"

"Aunt Irma—"

"—call him. Work it out. Don't let another day go by without—" The chime of the doorbell interrupted her. "Now, who could that be?" She smiled. Wide. "Maybe it's *him*."

Charlene rinsed her hands. "Oh, stop. Of course it's not." But just the thought that it might be had her pulse accelerating and her cheeks feeling warm.

The bell chimed again.

Irma said, "Would you like me to get it?"

"I'll do it." Charlene grabbed a towel and turned for the living room. "Check the green beans, will you? Don't let them boil over."

"Be happy to."

The bell rang a third time—a long, blaring chime. Whoever was out there was way too impatient.

Charlene rushed to the door and pulled it wide. Her sister was waiting on the other side.

Chapter Eighteen

"Hey," Sissy said.

Charlene could hardly believe her eyes.

Sissy wore a tight red skirt and a tube top. Her only jewelry was a giant-size pair of silver ear hoops.

Oh, God. Sissy. In the flesh, standing right there on her own front porch.

Sissy. At last.

"You gonna let us in?"

Us? Charlene had been so busy staring at Sissy, she hadn't even noticed the skinny guy with the tangled mass of black dreadlocks standing behind her.

"Hey," the guy said.

"This is Jet." Sissy stuck a thumb back over her shoulder.

Charlene pasted on a smile. "Hi, Jet." She felt rooted to the spot.

"Well?" Sissy demanded.

"Oh. Sorry. Sure..." She stepped back, and the two of them slouched into the foyer.

Sissy spotted the playpen and went right for it. She scooped the baby up into her arms. "How's my sweetie, huh? How's my darlin' Mia Scarlett?"

Mia giggled and cooed in Sissy's embrace, as if she knew her mommy. Sissy nuzzled her pink cheek and kissed her, making loud smooching sounds, rocking from side to side, whispering, "Oh, you are so sweet. Mommy's *so* glad to see you, Mommy has missed you *so* much...."

It was right about then that she caught sight of Irma standing in the arch to the kitchen, still holding her nearly empty glass of Cabernet. All the coos and baby talk stopped. "What the hell?" she muttered, her soft mouth curving into a sneer.

Irma said, gently, with a tender kind of sadness, "Sissy. I'm so pleased to see you're all right."

Sissy whirled on Charlene and spoke low and furiously over the patchy gold curls on Mia's head. "What's *she* doing here?"

"I live here," Irma said pleasantly before Charlene came up with an answer.

Sissy let out a low sound of pure outrage. "Here?" she demanded of Charlene. "With *you?*"

"No," Charlene told her. "She lives at the Sierra Star."

"For the time being, anyway," added Irma. "But I've bought a house on Commerce Lane. As soon as I've fixed it up, I'll be moving in there. Your Uncle Larry and I are divorcing."

"No..." said Sissy, still looking furiously at Charlene, showing Irma her back.

"Yes," said Irma. "I'm on my own and enjoying every minute of it."

Sissy let out a hard string of expletives. Mia, picking up her hostility, started to fuss. "Here," Sissy dangled the baby toward Charlene. "You'd better take her. She's used to you by now...."

Charlene was only too happy to get her arms around Mia again. She rocked her gently from side to side and the fussing stopped.

Sissy finally turned back to face Irma. "Look. I don't care why you're here. Just keep away from me, okay?"

"I'm so sorry you feel—"

"You ruined my life and you know it. I hate you."

"Oh, Sissy. If only—"

"Shut up," said Sissy. "I'm not here to hash out old times with you. Just keep the hell away from me, understand?"

"Yes. All right. If that's how you—"

Sissy chopped the air with a hand. "Just keep away. I mean it."

With a slow nod, Irma backed to the table and sat. She poured herself more wine, sighing heavily as she set the bottle down.

Charlene rubbed the baby's back and thought how much her aunt had changed.

Truly, *really* changed.

Charlene heard Irma let loose that sigh of resignation in the face of Sissy's bitterness and rage, and knew it had happened at last. Slowly, over time, with tenderness and love, her aunt had won her over. She'd come to trust Irma—to do the right thing. To be sweet and classy and fair and generous to a fault. And to sit down and be quiet when there was nothing else she could do.

The skinny guy spoke up then. "Sissy, let's get to it."

Get to what? Charlene cradled her niece close and tried to remember her manners. "We were about to have dinner. If you'd like to—"

"Forget dinner," Jet interrupted. "We're not here for that. We need to talk."

Charlene brushed Sissy's arm. "What's going on?"

Sissy wouldn't meet her eyes. "Sit down or something, okay? Jet'll explain."

"But—"

Jet cut her off. "Do like she said and sit your ass down."

Charlene's stomach churned. She felt…threatened, suddenly.

She cradled Mia closer and edged around the coffee table. "Okay, I'm sitting." She kept her voice level and looked squarely at Jet. "Explain."

"All right." Jet couldn't seem to keep still. He danced from one sneakered foot to the other. "All right. It's like this. That baby you got there? I'm her dad."

Oh, no… Charlene turned to Sissy. "Is that true?"

"Sure," Sissy said, too swiftly. "Yeah." She still wouldn't look directly at Charlene.

Anger bloomed inside Charlene, overwhelming her growing fear that her sister and this Jet character were up to no good. "Wait a minute." She kept her gaze on Sissy, daring her to meet her eyes. "What about Brand? I thought you claimed *he* was Mia's dad."

Jet grunted. "Who?"

Sissy let out a nervous titter of laughter. "Oh, that. I just did that to freak you out."

Charlene had suspected as much—but still. It hurt. A lot. To hear Sissy admit so offhandedly what she'd done, to hear her giggle about it as if it were some harmless prank. "How could you be so cruel—to me, or to Brand?"

Sissy had the grace to wince. But then she stuck out her lower lip in a sulky pout. "You always hated him. What do you care if he suffers a little?"

"It so happens I *don't* hate him. And whether I hated him or not, I care. Believe me. I really care."

"Don't look at me like that. It was only a joke."

"You see me laughing?" Charlene demanded.

Sissy sulked harder. "Well, and besides. Brand treated me like crap."

"Hey," said Jet, still bouncing around on the balls of his feet. "I'm tryin' to explain the situation here...."

Charlene ignored him. "Brand gave you a job. He tried to *help* you get started here in town when you swore no way you'd be working at the diner...."

"What?" Sissy whined. "All of a sudden you're on *his* side? He totally disrespected me, okay?"

"How?"

"Hey. Listen up," said Jet.

Charlene didn't so much as glance his way. She'd just put it together. Oh, she should have known. "You made a pass at him, didn't you? You threw yourself at Brand and he turned you down. So you trashed his office and ran off with the petty cash." *And he never told me. Because he knew how it would hurt me.*

At least her sister still had the grace to blush. Sissy threw up both hands. "Oh, so what? So I had a huge crush on him and he turned me down flat. So I thought I'd get myself a little revenge, get people talkin' about *him* the way they always whisper about me. So I made a mistake or two. Let's just forget about Brand for now, okay? He's not the father. He's really not. I admit I shouldn't have accused him.

I'm sorry I did it, okay? But he's got nothing to do with anything right now."

"Yeah," said Jet. "Can we get down to business here, huh?"

It was all way more than Charlene wanted to deal with. "What business?"

Jet cracked his knuckles. "It's real simple. We want—"

Charlene cut him off. "*I* want to hear it from Sissy."

Sissy was studying her shoes. "Jet will tell you," she mumbled out of the side of her mouth.

"Yeah," he said. "You're talkin' to *me*. So listen up. It's like this. I'm putting a band together, see?"

Mia was drooling. Charlene grabbed the diaper she'd left on the coffee table. Out of the corner of her eye, she saw Irma reaching for her purse.

"You listenin'?" Jet demanded.

She nodded. "A band?"

"Yeah. Rock and techno, with a reggae beat." Jet kept talking as Charlene smoothed the diaper on her dry shoulder and shifted the baby to that side. Over at the table, Irma rose from her chair and disappeared deeper into the kitchen, out of sight from the living room. Neither Sissy nor Jet seemed to notice. "Hey." Jet snapped his fingers at Charlene. "Pay attention. I'm talkin' here."

Charlene said, "I told you. I'm listening."

"Good. Because this is how it is. I'm headed for the big-time, ask anyone who's heard me play. And

Sissy and me, we know we're not cut out to be raising any kid. So it's like this. You give us ten thousand and we sign that kid over to you."

Surely Charlene hadn't heard him right. "Sign her over?"

"Whatever you call it." Jet feinted left and then right. Really, he looked like he was on speed or something. "You know. Like you can adopt her and we'll sign the papers all legallike, so she can be your kid."

Charlene glanced at her sister—who continued to stare at the floor. She couldn't believe Sissy would sink that low.

Neither could Irma, apparently. She slid into view again from somewhere over by the stove, her purse still clutched tight in her hands. "Oh, no. Sissy. You can't be serious."

Sissy glanced up then—just long enough to glare at Irma. "Shut up. I mean it. Stay out of this."

"Let's get this clear." Charlene spoke slowly and carefully. "You two are offering to…sell me your baby?"

"Call it what you want," growled Jet, still bouncing from foot to foot. "I get the money, you get the kid."

"Oh, no…" said Irma.

"Shut up," Sissy screeched at her.

Irma did what she was told. Charlene was quiet, too, cradling Mia close, glancing from Sissy to her hyperactive boyfriend and back to Sissy again.

The crazy thing—the terrible, sad thing—was that Charlene found herself tempted to agree.

She could get the money together. And Brand was a lawyer. He would know how to make it work—and funny, wasn't it? How he was the first person she thought of to go to for help, the first one she wanted to talk to about this?

Right now she longed to jump up and run out the front door. Run and run, holding Mia close—straight to Brand.

To talk it over. To ask his advice, to ask him to help her figure out what to do next.

Because she trusted him.

Again. At last. She did. She trusted him with her secrets. She trusted him to help her. She trusted him to be there when she needed him.

She trusted him with her heart.

"Well?" Jet demanded. "What do you say? Have we got us a deal or what?"

Charlene gaped at him. *This* was Mia's father? Oh, God...

Charlene ached for the innocent child in her arms. She ached for her sister, for this choice she was making that would haunt her for the rest of her life. "Oh, Sissy. How could you do this? How will you ever forgive yourself?"

"Listen to Jet," Sissy muttered. "That's how we do it. You deal with my man."

Her *man* kept talking. "We want the ten thousand

in the next twenty-four hours. And we want you to get a loan or something, give Sissy her half of the diner. Two hundred thousand. That's what we want for her share of that greasy spoon. We'll wait a week for that, for you to get a loan or whatever you have to do. But for the baby, we want ten thousand tomorrow. Got that? Tomorrow."

Charlene had heard about enough. "Sissy. Snap out of it. Tell this idiot he's crazy."

But Sissy, always the mouthiest, most indepen-dent of females, was now all about deferring to her *man*. "Just say yes, Charlene. Just do what he says."

In a pig's eye. "Forget about it," Charlene told Jet. "I'm not giving my sister a cent while she's under the influence of a creep like you."

Jet stopped bouncing from foot to foot. His thin face flushed red. "What did you say to me?"

"Let me make this very clear. No. I'm not *buying* Mia. And I'm not giving *you* anything for my sister's share of our restaurant."

"You're...not?" said Jet, as if he couldn't quite believe she would dare to simply tell him no.

"That's right. I'm not. And I want you to leave my house. Now."

Jet blinked. And then he sneered. "Fine. Whatever. We'll take you to court."

"Go for it."

"Fine. We will. You wait. Now, give us the kid."

"No."

"Huh? What do you mean, no? It's *our* baby. If you're not going to pay, you don't get to keep it."

Sissy looked up then. She darted a nervous glance at her hopped-up boyfriend. "Jet…"

"Quiet, babe," he told her. "I'm handling this." Charlene rose to her feet as he took a threatening step toward her. "Gimme that baby."

"No." Charlene backed around the end of the coffee table as Jet advanced from the other side. "No," she repeated. Softly. Clearly.

Jet pounced—too late. Charlene whirled and raced away, clutching Mia close. Behind her, she heard Jet swear. There was a sharp cry from Sissy. Mia let out a wail of frightened surprise.

Irma shouted, "You leave her alone, young man!"

Charlene reached the bathroom, darted in, shoved the door shut and engaged the privacy lock.

"Bitch! Let me in." Jet pounded on the door.

Mia wailed louder. Charlene rocked her and whispered gentle lies, "It's okay, honey. Okay. Okay…" as the SOB on the other side of the door pounded harder and called her more names.

The pounding stopped. Mia kept crying. Frantic, Charlene turned for the small window over the tub.

No way. It was too high up. She'd never get out with a baby in her arms.

Right then, something hit the door really hard. Charlene whirled on a gasp. She heard a hinge crack.

She backed up—all the way into the tub. Jet yelled

more obscenities—and threw himself against the door again.

That time the flimsy lock gave way. The door burst open and Jet burst in with it, the momentum carrying him so he banged the side wall along with the door.

Charlene cradled the sobbing baby close and wondered what in the world she was going to do next.

Jet righted himself and braced his skinny legs apart. He fisted those big-knuckled hands. "Gimme that baby. Now."

Charlene rocked the wailing Mia, pressed her lips hard together and shook her head.

Jet loomed toward her, fists raised—just as Sissy came flying in and grabbed his arm.

Tears streamed down her face. "Stop it, okay? Stop it, Jet. You just stop it now. This was a bad, bad idea. I don't want to go through with it. You leave my sister alone."

He tried to shake her off. "Lemme go. We're takin' that baby. She wants it, she can pay."

But Sissy held on tight. She shouted at him over Mia's wails of terror. "She's not your baby and you know she's not. Just forget it. I changed my mind. We're not doing this, after all."

He backhanded her.

She cried out as she fell against the sink, bringing up one hand to her flame-red cheek. "You bastard..."

He raised his arm to hit her again and she cowered back, wedging herself between the toilet and the sink.

Charlene shouted, "Stop!" as Irma appeared in the doorway clutching the big saucepan full of steaming hot water and green beans that Charlene had left on the stove.

"Stand back," said Irma, stepping between Sissy and Jet. Sticking an arm out to keep Sissy well behind her, she threw the contents of the saucepan at Jet.

He let out a yelp as beans and hot water went flying—landing mostly on him. Charlene whirled to face the far wall, using her body to shield the screaming, frightened baby.

Jet yelped some more, falling back against the door again, brushing wildly at his arms and chest and shoulders. "You burned me. You burned me!"

Charlene dared to turn back toward the crowded bathroom just as the front door across the small entry hall flew open.

It was Brand. Three long strides and he had her aunt gently by the shoulders. "Step back now, Irma. I'll take it from here."

Chapter Nineteen

Luckily for Jet, Irma had turned off the heat under the beans when he and Sissy arrived. He was burned but not seriously.

To be on the safe side, Brand called Brett after he talked to the sheriff's office. Brett and a deputy arrived at the same time. Brett did a little doctoring as the deputy started taking statements. An hour later, Jet sat in the back of the deputy's SUV on his way to the sheriff's station, where he'd be booked for assault and battery.

Brett left. And then Brand got up to go. Charlene had a million things to say to him. Too bad she didn't know how to begin.

So she thanked him. "I don't know what we would have done without you."

He smiled the smile that broke her heart. "Looks to me like Irma pretty much had things handled."

"Oh, yeah. She did great."

Irma had not only been real handy with that pan of beans, she'd also been the one who called Brand. She'd had the presence of mind to slide the cordless extension into her purse and duck out of sight to make the call.

"Lucky you had me on autodial," he said.

I love you. Oh, please. Give me one more chance. Let's try again. "Yeah," she said. "True. So lucky…"

"Good night, Charlene."

"Good night." She stood in the doorway and watched him get into his Jeep and drive away.

As she was shutting the door, Irma said tartly from behind her, "I can't believe you let him just leave like that."

Charlene turned around and grabbed her aunt in a tight hug. "You are amazing, you know that? Just flat-out, downright amazing."

Irma hugged her back. "Well, honey. I'd have to say the same for you."

Irma spent the night. Nobody slept until long after midnight. The three women had a lot of talking to do—a lot of plans to make.

Sissy cried a lot. No, she told them, Jet really

wasn't Mia's dad. Sissy hadn't even known him when she got pregnant—she'd only met him a couple of months ago, after she'd left Mia with Charlene. She admitted she didn't know who Mia's father was.

"There were…several guys, after I left town last year. It could have been any one of them. I was actin' up, goin' wild. But I promise you, I took good care of myself while I was pregnant. No drugs. No alcohol. I stayed at a women's shelter in the city until a couple of weeks after Mia was born. I was…proud, you know? That I was a responsible pregnant person, that Mia was born full term and healthy. But after a few weeks on my own with her…oh, I knew I wasn't makin' it. So I brought her to you, Charlene. I knew you'd take care of her. I knew you could give her the love and attention she needed…."

Sissy admitted she just wasn't sure about anything anymore. "I've made a mess of everything. I just don't know what to do. Everything I touch just seems to turn to crap."

Charlene grabbed her and hugged her and whispered that she should take it one day at a time, that nothing was so bad it couldn't be worked out.

Irma hugged her next. Sissy even hugged her aunt back. Strangely, she seemed to accept the change in Irma more easily than Charlene had been able to.

There was hope for her, for Sissy.

And as she watched her aunt comfort her sister,

Charlene just knew things were going to be better. Finally, her baby sister had opened up, let her hurt and confusion show. She had a long way to go, but she'd taken the first all-important step.

They began to talk of the future. Of how Sissy might begin to make a life she was proud of.

Irma revealed the truth about Uncle Larry. "That man ran my life," she said. "I never had time for you, Sissy, because all my energy was devoted to *him*. He wanted everything perfect and I worked so hard to make sure he got what he wanted." She touched Sissy fondly on the shoulder. And Sissy allowed the touch. "He agreed with me that it was our 'duty' to fight for custody of you—and then, when we won, he found you very inconvenient, a real person with needs and ideas of your own. I think he was actually happy that he and I had never had kids. And when you came along, he resented you right from the first. You were troubled and angry. You needed love and attention, and Larry never had much time for anyone but himself.

"And none of this, the hard truth about Larry, in any way excuses my own behavior toward you. I was a bad parent and I know it. I was living a big lie and all my energy went into keeping that lie alive." She spoke to Charlene. "Then, the day after I was so cruel to you on the phone, I dropped in at Larry's office unexpectedly—and found him with his pants down around his ankles."

"Oh. My. God," said Sissy. "He was doing that assistant of his, right? The cute one with the red hair?"

"Oh, was he ever. It was one of those moments a woman never forgets. I saw his bare bottom and that little redhead's legs wrapped around him and I thought, I've given up everything, destroyed my family, earned the hatred of both of my nieces, for *this?* I knew then I had to change, I had to do what I could to make up for the mess I'd made."

Charlene said, "You are doing one very fine job of it."

"Well, I'm working on it," Irma replied with a modest little smile.

At about 3:00 a.m., they finally called it a night. Sissy took the day bed in Mia's room, and Irma got a blanket and a pillow and fell asleep on the sofa.

Charlene lay in her own bed, wide awake, thinking of all that had happened—and longing for Brand. At quarter of four, she finally realized what she had to do. She got up and got dressed.

She was sneaking out the front door when Irma spoke from the darkness of the living room. "Going to see Brand?"

Sheesh. And she'd thought she was being so quiet. "Yes, I am."

"Good." Irma sounded more than satisfied.

"Go ahead and use my bed," Charlene suggested. "It's a lot more comfy than that cramped old sofa."

"Don't you worry about me, honey. Just go. He's one of the good ones. A real hero. You go to him. Now."

At Brand's house the entryway light was on.

He must have been awake, because she only had to ring the bell once and he was there, wearing red pajama bottoms and nothing else, looking like a dream walking—*her* dream.

The man she loved. The man she needed. The only man for her.

She whispered, "Couldn't sleep, either, huh?"

And he reached out and took her hand and pulled her over the threshold. He pushed the door shut and reeled her in.

Oh, it was the best place to be. The very best. Wrapped tight in Brand Bravo's embrace, his fine, warm mouth descending.

She raised her face to his kiss—a kiss as deep and sweet and arousing as any they'd ever shared.

When he lifted his head, she said, "I love you. I *trust* you. Tell me it isn't too late."

He said, "I love *you*. Always. Marry me."

"Yes," she whispered. "Oh, yes. I will."

"Forever?" He looked down at her, hazel eyes gleaming, kind of holding his breath.

As if he didn't quite dare to believe that they'd come this far. Together. The two of them. From young lovers, through heartbreak—to be enemies for so many years. And finally, to be friends again. Friends and more.

So much more.

"Charlene," he whispered. "Can you say it? Can you believe it at last? You and me. From now on…"

What a glorious moment. She'd never known the like. It was four in the morning on the sixth of July and they stood on the brink of the rest of their lives.

She said, "I've had a long talk with Sissy—and with Aunt Irma. Sissy wants to get her GED. She'll be living with Irma, taking it a day at a time. We agreed that Mia needs stability in her life and Sissy says she thinks it's for the best if I become Mia's legal guardian. Sissy will always be her mother, but this way she knows and *I* know that while she's finding her way in life, her baby will be safe. At least, that's what she said a few hours ago. You know how she is. I hope she doesn't change her mind."

"One day at a time," he said.

"Yeah. Right. Gotta remember that. And the thing with Jet does seem to have gotten to her. I think she really does want to change."

"You think she'd maybe consider a joint guardianship?"

It was just what she'd hoped he'd suggest. "You mean, you and I would be Mia's guardians, together?"

"Yeah." He framed her face, brushed her cheek with a tender kiss. "You and I…"

Funny how things worked out sometimes. Sissy had lied and named him as Mia's father. And now, in a sense, he *would* be.

"Oh, Brand. I think she might. I think she really wants to make things right, wants Mia to have the stability and love that Sissy lost when our parents died."

"Good, then. We'll talk to her."

"Yes. Okay. We will…"

"Say it, Charlene."

And she did. Proudly. Clearly. Looking right into his beautiful hazel eyes. "Absolutely. Forever. From this day forward, Brand. Oh, yes."

* * * * *

*Watch for the next installment
in the Bravo family saga,
A BRAVO CHRISTMAS REUNION,
coming in December
from Silhouette Special Edition.*

Mediterranean Nights

Join the guests and crew of Alexandra's Dream
*the newest luxury ship to set sail on the romantic
Mediterranean, as they experience the glamorous
world of cruising.*

*A new Harlequin continuity series
begins in June 2007 with
FROM RUSSIA, WITH LOVE
by Ingrid Weaver*

*Marina Artamova books a cabin on the luxurious
cruise ship* Alexandra's Dream, *when she finds out
that her orphaned nephew and his adoptive father
are aboard. She's determined to be reunited with
the boy…but the romantic ambience of the ship
and her undeniable attraction to a man
she considers her enemy are about to
interfere with her quest!*

Turn the page for a sneak preview!

Piraeus, Greece

"THERE SHE IS, Stefan. *Alexandra's Dream.*" David Anderson squatted beside his new son and pointed at the dark blue hull that towered above the pier. The cruise ship was a majestic sight, twelve decks high and as long as a city block. A circle of silver and gold stars, the logo of the Liberty Cruise Line, gleamed from the swept-back smokestack. Like some legendary sea creature born for the water, the ship emanated power from every sleek curve—even at rest it held the promise of motion. "That's going to be our home for the next ten days."

The child beside him remained silent, his cheeks working in and out as he sucked furiously on his thumb. Hair so blond it appeared white ruffled against his forehead in the harbor breeze. The baby-sweet scent unique to the very young mingled with the tang of the sea.

"Ship," David said. "Uh, *parakhod*."

From beneath his bangs, Stefan looked at the *Alexandra's Dream*. Although he didn't release his thumb, the corners of his mouth tightened with the beginning of a smile.

David grinned. That was Stefan's first smile this afternoon, one of only two since they had left the orphanage yesterday. It was probably because of the boat—according to the orphanage staff, the boy loved boats, which was the main reason David had decided to book this cruise. Then again, there was a strong possibility the smile could have been a reaction to David's attempt at pocket-dictionary Russian. Whatever the cause, it was a good start.

The liaison from the adoption agency had claimed that Stefan had been taught some English, but David had yet to see evidence of it. David continued to speak, positive his son would understand his tone even if he couldn't grasp the words. "This is her maiden voyage. Her first trip, just like this is our first trip, and that makes it special." He motioned toward the stage that had been set up on the pier beneath the ship's bow. "That's why everyone's celebrating."

The ship's official christening ceremony had been
held the day before and had been a closed affair,
with only the cruise-line executives and VIP guests
invited, but the stage hadn't yet been disassembled.
Banners bearing the blue and white of the Greek flag
of the ship's owner, as well as the Liberty circle of
stars logo, draped the edges of the platform. In the
center, a group of musicians and a dance troupe
dressed in traditional white folk costumes performed
for the benefit of the *Alexandra's Dream*'s first pas-
sengers. Their audience was in a festive mood,
snapping their fingers in time to the music while the
dancers twirled and wove through their steps.

David bobbed his head to the rhythm of the
mandolins. They were playing a folk tune that
seemed vaguely familiar, possibly from a movie
he'd seen. He hummed a few notes. "Catchy
melody, isn't it?"

Stefan turned his gaze on David. His eyes were a
striking shade of blue, as cool and pale as a winter
horizon and far too solemn for a child not yet five
Still, the smile that hovered at the corners of his
mouth persisted. He moved his head with the music,
mirroring David's motion.

David gave a silent cheer at the interaction. Hopefully, this cruise would provide countless opportunities for more. "Hey, good for you," he said. "Do
you like the music?"

The child's eyes sparked. He withdrew his thumb
with a pop. *"Moozika!"*

"Music. Right!" David held out his hand. "Come on, let's go closer so we can watch the dancers."

Stefan grasped David's hand quickly, as if he feared it would be withdrawn. In an instant his budding smile was replaced by a look close to panic.

Did he remember the car accident that had killed his parents? It would be a mercy if he didn't. As far as David knew, Stefan had never spoken of it to anyone. Whatever he had seen had made him run so far from the crash that the police hadn't found him until the next day. The event had traumatized him to the extent that he hadn't uttered a word until his fifth week at the orphanage. Even now he seldom talked.

David sat back on his heels and brushed the hair from Stefan's forehead. That solemn, too-old gaze locked with his, and for an instant, David felt as if he looked back in time at an image of himself thirty years ago.

He didn't need to speak the same language to understand exactly how this boy felt. He knew what it meant to be alone and powerless among strangers, trying to be brave and tough but wishing with every fiber of his being for a place to belong, to be safe, and most of all for someone to love him….

He knew in his heart he would be a good parent to Stefan. It was why he had never considered halting the adoption process after Ellie had left him. He hadn't balked when he'd learned of the recent claim by Stefan's spinster aunt, either; the absentee relative had shown up too late for her case to be considered. The adoption was meant to be. He and this child already shared a bond that went deeper than paperwork or legalities.

A seagull screeched overhead, making Stefan start and press closer to David.

"That's my boy," David murmured. He swallowed hard, struck by the simple truth of what he had just said.

That's my *boy.*

"I CAN'T BE PATIENT, RUDOLPH. I'm not going to stand by and watch my nephew get ripped from his country and his roots to live on the other side of the world."

Rudolph hissed out a slow breath. "Marina, I don't like the sound of that. What are you planning?"

"I'm going to talk some sense into this American kidnapper."

"No. Absolutely not. No offence, but diplomacy is not your strong suit."

"Diplomacy be damned. Their ship's due to sail at five o'clock."

"Then you wouldn't have an opportunity to speak with him even if his lawyer agreed to a meeting."

"I'll have ten days of opportunities, Rudolph, since I plan to be on board that ship."

* * * * *

*Follow Marina and David as they join forces
to uncover the reason behind little Stefan's
unusual silence, and the secret behind the death
of his parents....*

Look for From Russia, With Love
*by Ingrid Weaver
in stores June 2007.*

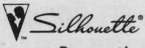

REQUEST YOUR FREE BOOKS!
2 FREE NOVELS PLUS 2 FREE GIFTS!

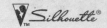

SPECIAL EDITION®
Life, Love and Family!

YES! Please send me 2 FREE Silhouette Special Edition® novels and my 2 FREE gifts. After receiving them, if I don't wish to receive any more books, I can return the shipping statement marked "cancel." If I don't cancel, I will receive 6 brand-new novels every month and be billed just $4.24 per book in the U.S., or $4.99 per book in Canada, plus 25¢ shipping and handling per book and applicable taxes, if any*. That's a savings of at least 15% off the cover price! I understand that accepting the 2 free books and gifts places me under no obligation to buy anything. I can always return a shipment and cancel at any time. Even if I never buy another book from Silhouette, the two free books and gifts are mine to keep forever.

235 SDN EEYU 335 SDN EEY6

Name _____ (PLEASE PRINT) _____

Address _____ Apt. _____

City _____ State/Prov. _____ Zip/Postal Code _____

Signature (if under 18, a parent or guardian must sign)

Mail to the **Silhouette Reader Service™**:
IN U.S.A.: P.O. Box 1867, Buffalo, NY 14240-1867
IN CANADA: P.O. Box 609, Fort Erie, Ontario L2A 5X3

Not valid to current Silhouette Special Edition subscribers.

Want to try two free books from another line?
Call 1-800-873-8635 or visit www.morefreebooks.com.

* Terms and prices subject to change without notice. NY residents add applicable sales tax. Canadian residents will be charged applicable provincial taxes and GST. This offer is limited to one order per household. All orders subject to approval. Credit or debit balances in a customer's account(s) may be offset by any other outstanding balance owed by or to the customer. Please allow 4 to 6 weeks for delivery.

Your Privacy: Silhouette is committed to protecting your privacy. Our Privacy Policy is available online at www.eHarlequin.com or upon request from the Reader Service. From time to time we make our lists of customers available to reputable firms who may have a product or service of interest to you. If you would prefer we not share your name and address, please check here. ☐

SSE07

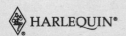

HARLEQUIN®

American ROMANCE®

**is proud to present a special treat this
Fourth of July with three stories
to kick off your summer!**

SUMMER LOVIN'
by
Marin Thomas,
Laura Marie Altom
Ann Roth

This year, celebrating the Fourth of July in Silver Cliff,
Colorado, is going to be special. There's an all-year
high school reunion taking place before the old
school building gets torn down. As old flames find
each other and new romances begin, this small
town is looking like the perfect place
for some summer lovin'!

*Available June 2007
wherever Harlequin books are sold.*

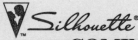

COMING NEXT MONTH